Yo-Yo

David Rolland

Jitney Books

#MADEINDADE

#MIAMIFULLTIME

To Everyone

Tuesday, September 20, 1988
12:59 p.m.
Chapter One

Henry James was a pencil pusher. No, he didn't sell pencils to math addicted children. He was an accountant for Friendly Bank. He double checked the balances and debits and it wasn't exactly how a young Henry would have pictured his life at 56, but it put food on the table. And without Henry none of this story would be possible. Eventually Henry will take some pride in that fact.

But on this day, Stan Friendly, the president of Friendly Bank saw Henry wasn't radiating his usual bliss. Stan walked toward Henry's desk and commented, "You're looking a bit down in the dumps."

"Am I? Sorry, Stan." Stan Friendly was the type of boss who liked to be addressed by his first name.

"No, I'm the one that's sorry, Henry. What's got you so down?"

Henry spoke into the light reflecting in his boss's shiny forehead. "I've had a lot on my mind. It's mostly my son. He graduated from college a couple months back and he moved back in with us. I thought we could help him get on his feet, but it's been three months and he hasn't done a thing. Nothing. Just watches TV and plays with his yo-yo."

"Yo-yo? Like the toy? That's not a pornographic reference is it?"

"No, no Stan. He's not a deviant. He's just got no ambition." Every word hurt so much for Henry to say. He had such high hopes for his boy.

Stan took a deep breath, a signal that let people know he was thinking deeply. "Is your son good with the yo-yo? Does he know any tricks?"

"He better. He spends all day playing with it. Why?"

"Just an idea. See, ever since Phil and Murray were nabbed by the Feds, I've wanted to improve the bank's image. I'm sick of Friendly Bank being thought of as the bank with Vice-Presidents who launder money. Now I got a plan, but your son had better be a heck of a yo-yo man." Henry didn't have time to ask what the idea might be because Stan continued, "If he's good we can book him for assemblies at the schools. He'll work a "say-no-to-drugs" message into it and we'll hand out yo-yos at the end that say 'Friendly Bank says no to drugs.' The community will eat it up. What do you think?"

Henry thought he better keep his opinions to himself. But it could get Benny out of the house. "I'll ask him tonight."

"You're not doing anything important, are you Henry? Go get him now."

And with that Henry left his air-conditioned workplace to see what his son was doing at one o'clock in the afternoon. Henry imagined his son perfecting his technique. Maybe one day Benny could be a motivational speaker? CEOs from across the nation would send their junior executives to hear Benjamin James spread wisdom with his yo-yo. Just like the magician at the accountants' conference motivated Henry last April.

But Henry was disappointed yet again. Instead of Benny preparing for a lucrative career of inspiring capitalists in the Tropics, his son was blasting loud rock n roll music while munching on a bucket of Crackerjacks. Henry couldn't put into words how let down he was that his son wasn't playing with his yo-yo. He sat next to Benny on the couch. Benny turned his head and asked, "Dad, why are you home so early?"

Henry turned off the music. "Benny, go shave and shower. I got you a job interview with Mr. Friendly."

"Right now? But I don't know what to say."

"Get cleaned up and put on some nice clothes and I'll tell you exactly what to do."

Benny followed his Dad's orders. He soaped up, dried off, combed his brown hair into a sharp part, put on clothes and clipped a bow tie under his chin. He greeted his Dad with a "What am I supposed to do?"

"You're going to shut-up, smile, and wow Mr. Friendly with your yo-yo tricks."

A quick drive and the father and son were back at the bank. Both of their hearts were shaking with nervousness. In the bank's lobby they saw Mr. Friendly chatting with a patron. Mr. Friendly made sure to smile and wave at Henry and Benny as they walked towards him. After laughing at a client's attempt at a pun Stan walked over to his accountant. "Henry! So this is your son. Hi, I'm Stan Friendly." Stan said as though they were never tied together in the three-legged race at the company picnic a couple years earlier. Stan put out his hand to shake. Benny took out his hand too, but not for a traditional handshake. Instead he lassoed Mr. Friendly's hand with his yo-yo, they shook and with a flick of his wrist, the yo-yo released Stan's hand and returned to Benny.

Flabbergastment.

Tellers stopped counting money. Kids stopped licking complimentary lollipops. Henry James wanted to know where his kid learned such awful job interview skills. Everyone was too shocked to talk but Stan Friendly. "That was amazing. Do you know any other tricks?"

Without a word Benny James pulled out half his repertoire. Around the world. Walking the dog. Rock the cradle. Sleepers. UFOs. All the easy tricks. But the applause was tremendous. A kid asked Benny for his autograph. Benny's little league coach when he was a kid patted his back. Stan Friendly wasn't a fool, he grabbed Benny leaving the audience wanting more. He took the father and son into the safety deposit room.

"Young man, how would you like to perform every Friday afternoon right here for a hundred dollars a show?"

"I'd love to, sir."

"I haven't finished yet. What's his name Henry?"

Benny answered for him. "It's Benny, sir."

"Don't call me, sir. Call me Stan. I'm also having you give inspirational speeches at the elementary school. I golf with the principal. He's always looking to book people for assemblies. I'll pay you $150 for the assembly. What do you think, Benny?"

"Sounds like a dream come true."

"Don't start waking up yet because I'm not done. I'm thinking world tours, tv specials, and maybe even a major motion picture."

"Are you joking?"

"Tell him, Henry, do I ever joke about politics, religion or making money?"

Henry chimed in, "Never, Stan."

Stan continued, "You might not know this Benny, but yo-yos used to be huge. Kids all over the world had them spinning around their fingers. There's just something about a yo-yo." Stan said as he held Benny's toy with reverence. "And all it will take is to watch someone like you to get all those kids now grown up to take out their yo-yos once again. Do you think you have what it takes?"

"Gee, I hope so."

Stan palmed Benny's yo-yo back to him with a handshake. They shook firmly as though a deal had just been struck. Then Stan let go.

"Well then Benny, go back out there and meet your public."

Benny walked out with his yo-yo jamming. Stan whispered in his accountant's ear. "Just you wait, Henry. I promise your son is going to be a star."

Tuesday, September 20, 1988
5:52 p.m.
Chapter Two

"Go ahead Benny, tell your mother what we did today."

Benny blushed as he served himself some sweet potato casserole. "Well, I got a job." He said with a hint of a smile.

"You did Benny! That's wonderful. Where are you working?"

"Man, Benny why didn't you tell me Kentucky Fried Chicken was hiring?" Jimmy laughed at his smart mouth comment. Jimmy, by the way, was Benny's punk seventeen-year-old little brother.

Benny was about to yell, but he calmed his rage with a sip of root beer. "Um...Dad took me over to Friendly Bank and Mr. Friendly... um... Stan.... He... uh.... hired me to do yo-yo tricks every Friday at the bank."

"Oh." Susan James said as she stared at her plate instead of her son. "Benny, you know your father and I didn't spend thousands of dollars for your college education so you could do yo-yo tricks once a week."

"No... yeah... I know, but like I'm also going to do school assemblies and... like it could lead to lots of other stuff."

Benny wanted nothing more than for this conversation to end. Same went for Dad and Jimmy, but Mom, she felt a point had to be made. "Benny, you've got to stop expecting things to fall into place for you. At some point you're going to have to start making things happen on your own. Your father and I weren't crazy when your sister joined the Peace Corps, but at least she's doing something with herself. Sitting around, working one hour a week..."

"For Christ's sake Susan," Dad pounded his hand on the table, "he got a job. It's a start. Let him enjoy it for at least tonight."

She backed off and dinner continued without any more conversation. After eating seconds, Benny excused himself. He walked upstairs and locked himself in his room. Then he sat on his bed and reread the letter the postman kindly delivered all the way from the Soviet Union.

Hey Bro,

Sorry it took me a while, but I finally found a pen and paper to write to you. Siberia is beautiful and even colder than you could imagine. The people are poor and my Russian is much worse than I thought. It's weird and lonely without you. What's the longest we've gone apart since we shared that space in Mom's womb? A month? Now we've got two years to finally become our own people. Unless you come visit (hint, hint). Write back soon and keep your chin up. Don't let any girl get you so down. Unless it's your awesome twin sister.

Xoxo,
Betty

Betty could always put a smile on Ben's face. Even from thousands of miles away. Mom always said Betty accidentally got both of their funny bones. Maybe Betty had taken his sense of purpose too. Benny couldn't imagine being motivated to pick up and move halfway across the world, not when he had trouble getting himself out of bed in the morning. Enough with the jealousy.

Ben started rehearsing for the big show on Friday. He thought about getting a fancier yo-yo. After all Michael Jordan never played basketball in worn down sneakers, but there was something about Benny's scratched up yo-yo that he never wanted to let go. He tenderly put his middle finger through the string's loop and everything felt right. Just a flick of the wrist and he had complete control. He could take it down. He could bring it back up. He could keep it floating in the air for incredible amounts of time. When Jimmy knocked on the door Benny wrapped the yo-yo around the doorknob and opened the door. Jimmy entered and Benny shut the door with his yo-yo, unwound the yo-yo from the doorknob and it came back to his hand.

After seeing Benny's complete mastery of the yo-yo for the first time, Jimmy's response was, "Holy moly, I didn't know you were that good with that thing."

Benny kept yo-yoing. "What do you want?"

"I… uh… let's go out Benny and celebrate your job."

"There's nothing to do in this stupid town."

"Shut up, Benny. Don't pretend you were Mister Cool in college. I bet you moped in your room all day there too."

Benny looked at his little brother and flicked his wrist. The yo-yo spun out of his hand at a painful speed. But Benny just wanted to scare his little brother, so he didn't smack him. He stopped the yo-yo's momentum a half inch from Jimmy's connecting eyebrows. Jimmy took a step back, but his big brother still didn't scare him.

"Let's go party you loser."

"You're not even 21, pimplebutt."

"I got a fake I.D…"

"But it's a school night. Mom won't let you out."

"Stop making excuses. I'll sneak out the window. Get dressed and I'll meet you outside in half an hour." And with that Jimmy left the bedroom. Benny went back to his yo-yo. The yo-yo was the only thing that made Benny's last two months bearable. All the uncertainty, the rejection, the loneliness, and his yo-yo has always been there. Its biggest impact was helping the time pass until something happened. With that toy five minutes could become half an hour, so Benny didn't have time to get spruced up before he ran outside to meet his brother. Jimmy waited for him in the front seat of their Mom's wood paneled stationwagon. Jimmy wore a flannel shirt to keep him warm and his hair greased back to keep him cool.

Benny got in the car and put his key in the ignition. "Don't tell Mom or Dad a word about this." Benny said in all seriousness.

"Yeah, that's the first thing I'll do smart guy. Tell Mom and Dad I snuck out on a school night."

Benny wasn't sure how enjoyable this night could possibly be. Arriving at an intersection he had to ask, "Where are we going?"

"To the only game in town. To Pretty Boy Floyd's." To emphasize how much fun they were going to have, Jimmy cranked up the radio. They drove past all the sights of Hatchet City. The school. Main Street. Friendly Bank. Then they made a left and there stood Pretty Boy Floyd's Bar and Grill. They parked between pick-up trucks and got out of the car. Benny had second thoughts about visiting this establishment. He'd heard the stories about the brawls, but he took a deep breath and opened the door to enter the infamous landmark for the first time. The music was pretty loud. The smoke was pretty thick. And the odor pretty ugly, but they stepped in anyway. An awful cover band was destroying the Doors' "Roadhouse Blues." Benny read the snare drum that screamed in bright red letters, "Hank and the Headband."

Jimmy yelled over the music into his big brother's ear. "You think this is bad. Wait until they play ZZ Top." They walked over to the bar. Jimmy sang along and more in key than Hank. "Save our city. Save our city. Right Now. You've got to roll, roll, roll…"

They waited patiently at the bar. Benny looked around and saw a lot of people he never wanted to associate with. Workers at the local factories. Out-of-shape ex-jocks who made fun of him in high school. But behind the bar he saw a girl that made the music sound beautiful. The smoke became a pleasant mist and that pretty, short haired blond that looked just like her was asking what they wanted to drink.

Jimmy had to answer for both of them. "Two ciders."

"Can I see some I.D., junior?" Jimmy pulled his fake one out. She looked it over. Benny handed his over, wishing there was a better photo of him on his driver's license. Shaving his head bald wasn't too flattering. She waved off his identification saying, "I know you're old enough." Then she filled a couple mugs from the tap. Benny fumbled with his wallet as he paid for their drinks. The brothers sat at the first open table they spotted.

"Wow!" Benny hollered.

"She's a beaut, huh?"

"Yeah." And Benny left it at that. He didn't go into how she was the spitting image of the only girl he ever loved. Back in college he went out with the most perfect gal in the world. She only wore black and liked poetry and liked Benny for four months exactly then got bored with his complete infatuation for her. But it couldn't be Kim. What would she be doing in Hatchet City?

"Her name's Jennifer Royce. Her little sister is in my biology class. She's a looker too." Jimmy said as he chug-a-lugged his drink.

"You should go talk to her. A small town girl's gotta be impressed with a big time college boy like you."

Benny knew his brother was messing with him, but it was worth a shot. Maybe after being around drunks all night she might be impressed by a Renaissance man. Someone who knows about yo-yos and how to build a house out of a deck of cards. Benny's tolerance for alcohol was so low that after one drink he started believing he had a chance with the prettiest girl in the bar. Even though she did reject him once before. But this wasn't Kim Feldman. This was Jennifer... something or other. Someone else, but it's Kim. Benny slammed down his mug and walked to the bar. He leaned against it and waited his turn while staring at Kim.

Fortunately she was tending bar so she assumed his look meant, "You want another cider?"

"Uh... uh..."

She went to the draft and filled another mug for him. "That's three dollars."

"Thanks... uh,... what's your name? Mine's Benny... Ben."

She took his money. "I know who you are. You were one of the twins two grades above me. My name's Jennifer. You don't remember me, do you?"

He really couldn't picture her face outside of college. She was Kim right down to the heavy eye make-up. But at that moment Benny couldn't remember how he got Kim to fall in love with him the first time. "Um... no. I don't remember you. But if you're two years younger, how can you work here?"

"Your brother's not the only one with a fake ID."

The band got really loud, so Benny had to start yelling. "What time do you get off work?"

"Why?"

"Since I graduated from college and moved back here... I don't... uh.... Maybe we could talk or...."

She smiled.

"I get off at 2:30 usually. What did you study in college?"

"Um... Communications."

And she laughed. Benny wasn't sure if she was laughing with him or against him. Either way he walked back to his seat feeling like a champ. Jimmy was sitting down laughing too. Benny knew he couldn't have overheard the conversation, so he asked, "What's so funny?"

"The singer. He dances like a goon." The singer, Hank, was shaking his head up and down. He looked like a chicken that thought its head got cut off. "So how did it go? I saw you charming her."

"She… uh… wants to meet up at 2:30. After work."

"Oh, man. 2:30? You dog, you." Jimmy laughed as he rubbed his two index fingers at his naughty older brother.

Benny now remembered how easy it was to get a superiority complex in this tiny town. They made more fun of the band, inhaled more second-hand smoke, and Benny handed the keys to the car over to his baby brother. Jimmy drove home to get a few hours of sleep before school and Benny figured he could get a ride from Kim… no Jennifer. "Don't you dare call her Kim," Benny told himself, "Or you'll have to walk the two miles home."

Benny heard Hank and the Headband play every god awful song in their repertoire. He heard Kim yell, "Last call." He heard the big bouncer command, "Everybody out." From outside he heard sweeping and he came back in. Kim was counting the money. Benny stepped over broken glass to get to her.

But that big, bearded bouncer got in his face.

"Hey, we're closed."

Benny was still too timid to stand up for himself, so Kim had to save him. "Don't worry Bobby. He's with me." After giving Ben a harsh look, the bouncer walked away. Kim explained, "He's a bit protective of me…" She didn't finish the thought, but she did finish counting the bills. She then grabbed her coat and they stepped outside. "I can't stay out too late. I need to check up on my Baby."

"You've… you've got a kid?"

She nodded her head. "You've got a problem with my Baby?" Benny didn't know exactly how to respond until she broke into laughter. "I'm just foolin'. I'm one of only twenty girls in my graduating class that haven't gotten knocked up yet. I have a cat. His name's Baby. What do you want to do?"

"Um… what do you want to do?"

"You must have had some plan when you invited me out." Then she laughed again. "But maybe I don't want to know what you were planning? Come on, we'll get some coffee."

They got into her tiny Toyota and drove to the 24 hour convenience store. He wanted to apologize for being so intrusive in the past, but then he remembered she's not the same girl, so Jennifer started the conversation. "How's your twin sister? Is she back in town too?"

"No. Betty joined the Peace Corps. She's in Siberia teaching English and other things."

"Wow!" Jennifer was impressed. "So why did you come back to Hatchet City?"

"I don't know. I didn't know what to do, so I figured I'd come back home and save up some money."

"Once I leave this town, I'm never coming back. You got a job?"

"Yeah… I just got hired by Mr. Friendly…. Stan… over at Friendly Bank.'

"You're going to be a banker?"

"No. I'm going to be doing… um…. Yo-yo tricks."

She cracked up with laughter. "That's awesome. That's the best job I've ever heard. You're really good with the yo-yo?"

"Um…. Yeah… I guess." He wasn't comfortable with all the attention. He changed the conversation's focus back to her. "What do you… um… do, besides work at Pretty Boy Floyd's."

She parked the car. The store's neon lights reflected against the windshield. "I take acting classes over at Hatchet City Community College. I hope to move out to LA or New York to become an actress."

Benny took a breath of relief as they entered the processed food heaven. Finally a noticeable difference between her and Kim. Kim hated theater people. They never knew when to stop the theatrics. Benny and Jenny filled paper cups with brown liquid posing as coffee. Then they poked fun at all the ridiculous products for sale. Clam juice. Beef jerky in a can. Sunglasses in the shape of cartoon characters. "You know what I hate about people our age?" Jennifer answered without giving Ben a chance to reply. "We all expect to bond over pop culture. It's stupid. This one guy in class said to me, 'Oh my God, you like Scooby-doo too? We must be soul mates.' Just because we like to shut off our brains to the same entertainment, doesn't mean anything. You know?"

"I guess."

"Oh! Look, a yo-yo. You've got to do some tricks for me." She walked to the cashier and paid for their coffees and the yo-yo. She insisted it was her treat since he was going to perform for her. She sat on the curb and said, "Entertain me."

Benny cracked open the package. He was a bit wary since the night air stiffens up finger joints. Plus, she bought a garbage, plastic yo-yo and the string was too long and the yo-yo didn't have much kick. "I wish I had my yo-yo here. This one's kind of third rate."

"No excuses."

No excuses. He knotted the loop for his middle finger. He let the yo-yo dangle to the ground, so the string could straighten itself out. Then he wrapped it back up. He gave the yo-yo a trial run, but it just wouldn't give. He threw it down and then back up. Down and back up. Then he kept the yo-yo down for fifteen seconds. "This is a sleeper." He pulled the yo-yo back up. It went back down again and he walked as the yo-yo rolled against the ground. "Now I'm walking the dog." Back up it went. Then he flicked it back down again with his right hand, grabbed half-way down the string with his left hand making a nice little loop which the yo-yo swung back and forth through. "This is rocking the cradle."

She stood up and tisked, "I know all these tricks. Don't you have any that you've made up on your own?"

He twisted the yo-yo back up and smiled. "I got this one called, 'nabbing the girl'"

"Nabbing?" she halfway questioned until she saw him sidearm toss the yo-yo. The string wrapped around Jennifer and then around Ben. They were tied together like a little Christmas present. Before they could get too intimate, he unwrapped them, so the yo-yo came back to his hand. Thereby completing the trick.

"That was cool," she said. "Can you do it again? I think you forgot a step to it."

He tied her to him again and asked, "What did I forget?"

She silenced him with a cold lipped kiss. They continued smooching even as Benny untied them to get the yo-yo back to his hand, so the trick was complete. When their lips separated, Jennifer asked, "You still can't remember me?"

"No. Not the way you think I should." He then kissed her passionately so he wouldn't need to explain.

Friday, October 7, 1988
3:58 p.m.
Chapter Three

All over Hatchet City posters were proclaiming, "Friendly Bank proudly presents The Yo-Yo King." There was a picture of Benny spinning his yo-yo towards the outside world. Underneath the photo there was more text. "Local legend Benny James will wow you and kapow you with his complete mastery of the yo-yo. Free admission. Starts 4:00 sharp at Friendly Bank."

It was the talk of the town. At least in Benny's mind. Stan had created the expectation that all of Hatchet City was preparing to see the greatest show on Earth. So Benny was having trouble breathing. He was in the bank's men's room minutes before he was supposed to perform. Jen entered as he was pouring water on his face. "You're going to be great. And this time you've got your real yo-yo."

He muttered inaudibly, "Thanks Kim." But it sounded like, "Thanks, hmmmm." She still hadn't noticed he wanted her to be someone else. She gave him one last peck on the cheek while Stan popped his head through the door.

"You ready, kid? I'm going to introduce you in five minutes."

Benny nodded his head because he was still too terrified to speak. He waited around the corner out of sight giving his trusty wooden yo-yo a couple practice spins as he heard Stan warm up the audience. Benny could hear the two foot smile on Stan's face. "Good afternoon ladies and gentlemen, boys and girls, I along with the rest of the Friendly Bank family want to thank you for coming out here and sharing your willingness to be befuddled. You are in for a treat as the legendary Benny James is going to amaze and start a craze. After the show I'm sure you're all going to want your own yo-yos. All you have to do is start a savings or checking account and.... Well, we can talk about that after the show. Let's bring out the one... the only ... Benny James."

Benny couldn't think up a glamorous entrance, so he just jogged out there with a nervous limp to his step. He pressed his back against the tellers' counter. "Thanks Mr. Friendly... um... Stan. Hi everybody. How are you all doing?" his voice cracked. There weren't as many people as he expected. Three rows of children sitting with their legs crossed with the Moms sitting behind them. All the bank employees including his Dad were there. His Mom came, so did Jennifer and a couple of old folks, but not too many other people. Of course, even without a massive crowd, he was still tense.

His first trick, the sleeper, didn't sleep for too long which added to his nerves. Especially since no one oohed or ahhhed to it. So he tried it again and the silence was deafening. "This trick is called the sleeper... um... because it's really boring and it puts everyone to sleep." They all laughed which made his job a little easier. He continued his repertoire, escalating the level of difficulty with each new trick. He kept sneaking a peek at his girl. She got kind of dressed up for him in her black dress. The only other time he saw her in such fancy clothes was back in college when she dragged him to an opening night performance of the college dance troupe's version of Swan Lake. It was her favorite ballet and she kept on thanking him for being a sport and coming along with her even though it was the most boring thing in the world.

Benny smiled at Jennifer as he did the spinning trick he called "The UFO." He wondered if she was thinking about that same magical moment. Jennifer smiled back at him, so he was sure they were sharing a thought. Don't tell Ben, but Jennifer was only thinking about how goofy her new boyfriend looked with a bow-tie and a yo-yo. As Benny finished making his yo-yo look like a UFO, Stan grabbed Benny's yo-yo and yelled, "Isn't that amazing? How about a big round of applause for Benny James." Everyone clapped fairly enthusiastically. "Now if you're interested in signing up for an account for your free yo-yo, tellers are standing by."

As everyone got up Stan whispered into Benny's ear, "Wait in my office. I want to talk to you."

Benny walked past well-wishers and congratulators into the nether realm of Friendly Bank. He entered the office and studied the pictures on Stan's desk. There were photos of Stan's ex-beauty queen wife. A picture of Stan's daughter in a junior Miss Hatchet City beauty contest tiara. Then there was a picture of a middle-aged man with a big nose shaking hands with Jimi Hendrix.

The door opened and shut. "What the heck was that? That was the most boring fifteen minutes of my life."

"Well sir, you stopped me before my best two tricks."

"Don't you dare call me sir. Call me Stan. And you would have just wasted those tricks. Your mind wasn't there today. There was no passion. No creativity. When you came in here last week and shook my hand with your yo-yo, there was passion. There was creativity. There was magic. But obviously someone poured LSD in my coffee that morning because I must have been hallucinating. Here…" He counted out some twenties and threw them in Benny's face.

Benny counted the money and put it in his pocket. "I'm sorry … sir… uh… Stan to disappoint you." Benny was heartbroken and got up to leave.

"Aww kid. Get back in here. You're just like your Dad. You are too thin skinned. You've got to relax." Stan combed his hair over his tiny bald spot. "I just thought you'd be a star right away. You know, the Friendlys haven't always been into banks."

"No?"

"No. My Daddy, Stan Sr., opened Friendly Bank back in 1955. He got the capital from my grandfather, Lenny Friendly. Grandpa Lenny used to manage a lot of vaudeville acts."

"What's vaudeville?"

"You're vaudeville kid. Vaudeville is theater for the people. Ventriloquists, comedians, strong men, yo-yo men. That's all vaudeville. You'll have to come over for dinner one night and watch some of the old films. Anyway, while my Dad was forming the bank, his brother, Morie, was following in Grandpa's footsteps. He became a concert promoter. Booked all the big acts into Detroit. The Beatles, Bob Dylan, Jimi Hendrix. And then two hours before a big Kiss show that Uncle Morie booked was going to start, he died at age 48 of a heart attack. They dedicated the show to him."

"I'm sorry Stan."

"Don't be. I just didn't have anyone to lead me into the entertainment business, so I took over the bank when Dad retired. Fell in love, got married, had a daughter and fell in love again. I just thought Benny that you had the drive to push me back into the family business."

"What could I do to make the show better?"

"Put some energy into it. I want to see two or three yo-yos going at the same time. I want to see the impossible. You're going to do that Say No to Drugs assembly at the elementary school next week and I want to smell the electricity in the air. I want you to make the whole audience, the kids, the teachers, the cafeteria ladies, wish they were you. Now go home and practice."

Benny ran out of there with one thing on his mind. Kim.

Friday, October 14, 1988
9:45 a.m.
Chapter Four

"Ha ha ha."

"What are you laughing at?" Benny asked his little brother. They were both sitting behind the wool curtain of Hatchet City Elementary School's stage. The school's stage was in the cafeteria, so the slight stench of that coming afternoon's sloppy joe lunch permeated the air.

Jimmy smirked. "This is awesome. I should be in economics class right now." Jimmy was referring to the fact that his big brother arranged an excused absence for him. Benny needed some actors for his performance, so Jimmy volunteered his time. Not only did he get out of school legally, he also got community service hours all those colleges were supposedly looking for.

Jennifer also got dragged into the assembly, but she was enjoying it for different reasons than Jimmy. She loved to act and she recited her lines with some real gusto. Her pacing was making Benny nervous though as was the new yo-yo he bought. Oh, he still had his trusty wooden yo-yo on his right hand, but for his left hand he bought an unproven yo-yo. It felt fine, but it hadn't been battle tested. Nor had his left arm been pushed to the extreme. Benny made a mental note that if he was going to take his yo-yo career seriously, he needed to start implementing an exercise regiment. Turn his body into granite and build endurance, so he could do six exhibitions in one day if need be.

Benny, Jimmy, and Jennifer heard footsteps on the other side of the stage. Benny told his co-stars, "Alright guys, get in your places."

On the other side they heard an authoritarian lady speak into a microphone. "Hello everyone. We've got a treat for you today. As part of Say No to Drugs Week, we brought an example of how great your lives can be if you just... everybody now..."

A lot of young voices screamed in unison, "SAY NO TO DRUGS!"

The speaker continued. "Yes, so we've got a young man who graduated from this school eleven years ago. He recently graduated from college but moved back to Hatchet City to give back to the community. But before we begin, remember, you are all young adults, so please do not throw anything or yell at our guests. Here he is… Benny James."

The curtain slowly slid open. Benny glanced out at a cafeteria filled with young boys and girls seated in blue, plastic chairs. He panicked because his music wasn't playing, but then it did. An energetic disco beat and Benny started circling his yo-yos all over the place. He flipped it through his legs, behind his back and around his belly, then he unwound it back to his hand. "How's everybody today?"

No one said a word. So Benny yelled louder, "How's everybody doing today?"

"Good." Some kids said, though all their eyes were on the yo-yos dancing in the air.

"You know why you're feeling good? Because you didn't do drugs today. You know why I'm feeling good?" He did a sleeper with the left yo-yo while the right yo-yo wrapped itself around it. "Because I said no to drugs today. And I say no to drugs everyday. Otherwise I couldn't do all these neat tricks. If I did drugs I couldn't focus on what's important. My friends. My family. My yo-yo."

Off cue Jimmy walked on to the stage. He was wearing a black, leather jacket. Jennifer put powder on his face and black lines under his eyes to give him a junkie aura. He pointed a cigarette and lighter at Benny. "Hey man, do you want to smoke some pot?"

"No." Benny yelled and with one yo-yo he knocked the cigarette and lighter out of Jimmy's hand. With the other yo-yo he lassoed Jimmy's legs and crashed him to the ground. A little violence was all it took to get the kids' attention. "The yo-yo was originally designed by the Chinese as a weapon. A weapon against drugs. But yo-yos aren't the only weapons against drugs. Do you kids know any other weapons?"

"Guns."

"Bazookas."

"Grenades."

Benny wasn't prepared for those answers. "No, I don't mean like that. I meant sports, music, school. Skills that you can spend your time perfecting instead of wasting your time killing brain cells with drugs. See, I could never do this trick, the UFO, if I did drugs instead of practicing."

"Wow dude, a UFO." Jennifer came onstage in a ripped t-shirt sounding convincingly like a junkie.

"Excuse me Miss, why do you do drugs?"

She sobbed, "Because my life is empty and I have nothing except for my heroin."

Without a word he tied her up with his yo-yo and pulled her towards him. He told her, "Get that needle out of your hand and replace it with a yo-yo." He took out a blue, plastic yo-yo from his pocket. "Friendly Bank" was written on its side. Jennifer put it around her finger and did the two tricks Benny had taught her. "Wow! This is so much groovier than heroin!"

He asked the audience, "Alright, does anyone else want to learn how to yo-yo?" Half the kids raised their hands. Benny picked the six nerdiest looking kids. He didn't want any class clowns coming up there and pulling down his pants. He gave the kids yo-yos and started showing them how to walk-the-dog.

Stan Friendly then made an unbilled appearance on stage. "Kids, wasn't that great?" The response was pretty boisterous. "Would you kids all like to get your own yo-yos?" They all screamed. "Well, all you have to do is prove you're drug free. We've got nurses here who are going to collect urine samples from you. Come up clean, you get a free yo-yo."

The whole cafeteria could hardly contain itself. They clapped loudly as Benny, Jimmy, and Jennifer walked off stage. Stan whispered into Benny's ear, "You're getting better kid, but you still need work. Come to my house around six-ish tomorrow and we'll talk."

The three performers exited out the side door. Jennifer whelped out a loud, "Man that was awesome." She kissed Benny's neck. "You were great. You really showed Friendly who the man is. All that dialogue you wrote came out great. All that tongue in cheek cheesiness was the best."

Benny smiled at both her stick-it-to-the-man attitude and her adoration. They got in her car, but from the backseat Jimmy had to chime in, "I hate to break it to you, Jen, but that's how Benny thinks people talk. Your boyfriend's a real square."

"Thanks Mr. Hip," she said back. "Oh look at the time, we can drop you back at school in time for third period."

She started driving towards the high school. Jimmy begged and pleaded all the way to school, but they wanted to be alone. After Jimmy was kicked out of the car the young couple continued driving toward Hucaloosa Park. They walked under the falling leaves to a secluded spot where no one would bother them.

Out of nowhere Jen dragged Ben down to the ground with her. After a moment of kissing she rested her head on his lap and asked, "Wasn't that weird going back to the elementary school?"

"You went to Hatchet City Elementary too?"

"Yeah, I grew up here. God, I can't believe you really don't remember me. I thought you were just trying not to embarrass me."

He rubbed her tummy. "I'm sorry. I just didn't pay attention to too much when I was a kid. Besides you were two grades below me."

Tears were gently rolling out of her eyes. "You don't remember your senior year? When there were drawings of me all over school kissing Jessica Sayles? You never heard all the stories about me?"

"No, I never paid any attention to that. Are the stories true?"

She looked at him, shook her head and laughed. "Man, I'm so glad you can make me laugh. No, I only like boys." And she kissed him to back it up. "I especially like boys who tell bullies to leave me alone back when I was just a defenseless young girl, like you did even though you don't remember it."

"I really did that?" Benny was shocked by his own nobility. "Why would anyone tell lies about you?'

"It was just a slumber party. We were playing truth or dare and my dare was to kiss Jessica. The story grew and grew and whatever… that's not important. What is important was for every bad person, there's a good person out there. That you would stand up for someone who felt like the whole universe was against her, it meant the world to me. It still does." She kissed him with passion.

Benny kissed her back, but with a different energy. One of suspicion and guilt because that story did not sound like one that would come out of the mouth of Kim Feldman.

Sunday, October 23, 1988
5:37 p.m.
Chapter Five

After much fighting and debating, it came down to a coin toss as to whether Benny got the car or his Mom. "Call it in the air," she said.

"Tails." Benny yelled. But tragically George Washington's head faced the sky. "But Mom I need the car tonight."

"So do I Benny, but I won the coin toss fair and square."

He bent down to pick the coin off the ground. "Alright I'll just look so stupid and unprofessional being dropped off by my Mom. Hey…" After careful inspection of the coin Benny noticed "There's no tails. This is a two headed coin."

"Well, you're the one who called tails, honey. Go get dressed and I'll drop you off."

Benny cursed his luck to be born to a cheating Mom. He slipped into a recently ironed pair of khakis and a blue-gray button-down shirt. He stuck the yo-yo in his pocket just in case he might need it and out he went in the crisp autumn air.

On the drive Benny came to a realization. "Why did Dad need the car tonight?"

"He said he was going to a movie." Benny thought that was a bit out of character, so Mom explained, "I think, dear, your father is a little hurt that Stan invited you over for dinner."

"Why?"

"Your father's worked for Stan Friendly for ten years without a dinner invitation. You got one right after meeting the man."

As though Benny's knees weren't shaking enough from having to eat dinner with adults, now Benny felt parental pressure too. He tried relaxing by looking at all the nicely manicured lawns of Hatchet City, but all he could think about was how calm he would be if Kim was with him. Then the car stopped. They were in front of Stan's house so Mom said, "Make sure to call when you need to get picked up. And don't stay out too late. Your sister is supposed to call at eight in the morning."

Benny felt awful. For a couple days now he had forgotten that he had a twin. Betty was no longer around to remind him that he didn't enter this world alone. Benny stopped thinking about his sister and rang the bell which made a very majestic "Doing." Footsteps approached and Stan Friendly was at the door. "Ben! Right on time. Come on in." Benny wiped his penny loafers on the doormat, so he wouldn't stain the marble floors. Every luxury imaginable was displayed in Stan's home. A wide screen TV. A giant whirlpool in the bathroom. A state of the art microwave in the kitchen operated by Stan's wife.

"It's a pleasure to meet you Mrs. Friendly."

She pointed her shiny red fingernail at him. "Now Ben, you better start calling me Cindy or there's going to be trouble."

Next Ben got to meet their daughter, Veronica. After all the introductions they sat in the dining room for dinner. Sirloin steaks. Red wine. Key Lime Pie. The works. After Ben couldn't eat a smidgen more, Veronica excused herself to do some homework and Cindy started bringing the dishes into the kitchen. So it was just Ben and Stan with his canary eating smile sitting at the table.

Benny complimented his host. "That was some meal, Stan. Your wife is a heck of a cook."

"She sure is." Stan lit up a cigar, but Benny was the one hacking and choking. "But I didn't invite you over to fatten you up or to hear your flattery. I wanted you to see something." Stan got up. It was painstakingly obvious that Benny was supposed to follow. But first Benny loosened his belt a notch to get a little breathing room. Stan continued his commentary, "My daughter saw you at the elementary school. She was impressed, but I didn't see her running home to play with her yo-yo. So you've still got a lot of work to do on showmanship and getting an audience to fall in love with you."

They entered a dark room which was no longer dark when Stan flicked the light switch. There was a giant screen against the wall and a projector in the back. There were three rows of couches and in the front one Stan insisted Benny to, "Have a seat, my boy. You're in for a treat.

My Grandpa Lenny filmed some of the entertainers he represented and from them you're going to learn how to work a crowd. Hit the lights, will you?"

Benny did as he was told. The room was dark and a chua-chuka-chuka-chuka sound like a locomotive came from the projector. The footage was kind of grainy, but Benny could still make out a massive, shirtless man walking up the steps to a wooden stage. Stan wouldn't keep quiet. "Now there's no sound to these films, but the fact that these fellows are still so darn entertaining shows the importance of stage presence. Look... see how that strongman is struggling to lift that horse. That's Gregor the Gigantic. My Grandfather said he could lift two horses easily, but by making what he does look difficult he engages the audience. When you come on stage so smug, making your tricks look easy as pie, the audience thinks you're a jerk. But if you come out there looking nervous telling the crowd this trick had only been completed once in the history of humankind, the audience gets on your side."

Benny understood what Stan was getting at. And for a while he found the films and Stan's point by point commentary somewhat interesting. But reel after reel after reel after reel of chicken eating geeks, men who shot themselves out of cannons, and double-jointed pretzel ladies compounded with hours of the only sounds being from the projector and the all knowing wisdom spewing from Stan's mouth was driving Benny mad. Benny was ready to ask for a bathroom break when something caught his eye. In glorious black and white stood a young man. He was slim and slender hiding his true face under a Lone Ranger mask. A cape was on his back, and the kid was mysterious enough to pull it off without looking ridiculous. "Stan. Stan, who is this guy?"

"I'm not sure. I never watched this reel before.... Oh Jesus." Stan was speechless. Ben was even more flabbergasted because what came out of the kid's hand but a yo-yo. He created spirals, made flowers out of his string, he pretended the string was spaghetti and ate it. It was magic and it was perfect and it was too fast because before they could be sure they were seeing what they were seeing, the star grappled his yo-yo around a tree branch and swung off-screen like he was Robin Hood.

"Stan, we've got to find out who that was. That was unreal. I didn't know the yo-yo could do some of those things."

"I'm looking kid. I'm looking." And Stan scanned the film cans. He was always desperate for things he didn't have. "Here it is... the Yo-Yo Kid. That's it? No real name... no... aah I got it." Stan left the projector going and walked out of the room. Ben was quick to follow him through the living room and into a walk-in closet. The room was filled with file cabinets and women's shoes. Stan searched through one cabinet and then another and then "Aha!" he exclaimed. He took out a dusty folder and explained, "I've kept a hold of all of Grandpa Lenny's business transactions. That film was taken in 1927 so..." He stopped explaining, licked his finger and searched through all the yellowed documents. After a few pages his eyes lit up. He started reading, "I, Simon Wiesel, also known as the Yo-Yo Kid agree to be managed and represented by Lenny Friendly. For a small percentage, to be decided later, Lenny Friendly agrees to direct your career. The name, the Yo-Yo Kid, will be maintained and owned by Lenny Friendly to make certain it is not abused. The name, the Yo-Yo Kid, along with any profit making enterprises Simon Wiesel has with his yo-yo will be represented by Lenny Friendly."

Stan sounded slightly embarrassed by his grandfather's obviously abusive contract. He searched through more papers because there had to be more about Simon Wiesel, The Yo-Yo Kid. There was more. There was a motion picture deal with MGM where the Yo-Yo Kid agreed to star in three pictures. Has the World Gone Yo-Yo?, The Yo-Yo Kid Meets Dracula, and another picture to be named later. Then there were contracts signed for the Yo-Yo Kid's paid endorsements of Yum-Yum, the chocolate yo-yo.

As the years went on they found more papers detailing the career of Simon Wiesel. The last one was dated June 13, 1931. It read, "Dear Mr. Wiesel, Please be advised that we are bringing suit against you for an amount of ten thousand (10,000) dollars for behavior which has been detrimental to the valuable name of the Yo-Yo Kid. Upon receipt of this letter, you are to cease and desist using the name the Yo-

Yo Kid, nor are you to perform in public using a yo-yo. Sincerely, J. Peter Solomon."

"Jeez! What do you think he did Mr. Friendly?"

"I don't know, but that seems to be the last document concerning Wiesel. But from what I can tell, as the rightful heir to Lenny Friendly, I own the name, the Yo-Yo Kid. So how would you like that to be your new handle?"

Benny thought it over. "Well, I'm 22. I'm not sure I'm a kid anymore. Besides how do you think Simon Wiesel would feel when he hears someone else is using his name?"

"I'm sure the old man is as dead as a..." For once Stan Friendly was stuck. All of this new information had temporarily robbed him of the ability to conjure up metaphors on the spot. "Well, I'm sure he's dead, but be my guest. Try to dig up the old pro and get his approval. But don't spend too much time looking. We got the Amateur World Yo-Yo Championship in Chicago coming up soon."

"But you've been paying me. Doesn't that mean I'm a professional?"

"You crack me up kid. Haven't you noticed me paying you under the table? Now get out of here and go look up your eighty-year-old legend."

Benny could tell that was his cue to leave. He was too shy to ask if he could use the phone to call for a ride. So he took the long walk home under the stars. Glad as could be that he brought his yo-yo, to keep him company.

Thursday, February 16, 1988
12:21 p.m.
Chapter Six

It was lunchtime. Jennifer cooked up a can of barbecued beans. They tasted alright, just a little bit monotonous. By the twentieth spoonful Benny had lost his appetite. The next day he was leaving for Chicago. The big Amateur World Yo-Yo Championships and Convention. Jennifer was a little glum since she wasn't coming along.

"Why don't you just come then?" Benny pleaded as he pushed his bowl of beans away.

"I can't miss work and I've got rehearsals over the weekend too. Besides it isn't that. It's that we never talk any more."

Never talk? Kim never cared whether they talked. She knew she was just supposed to cheer him up by pointing out rainbows in the horizon.

Jennifer continued her diatribe. "I mean we've been going out for almost five months and I don't feel like I know you at all. All we talk about is Simon Wiesel and whatever else doesn't have anything to do with you."

"Ask me whatever you want."

"Do you love me?"

No. He loved Kim Feldman and Jen obviously was not her. "Yeah." Truth is overrated.

"Have you been in love before?"

This time he did tell the truth because any time he had a chance to talk about the greatest time in his life, he would. "Yeah, in college there was a girl I loved very much. She didn't love me and it ruined my life until I met you."

She smiled. All that time around Stan had taught Benny how to tell people what they want to hear. The fine art of manipulation. "How did it ruin your life?" she asked.

"Well, I was about to graduate from college and my only plan for the future was to have my life revolve around her. That scared her and she said she didn't want to see me anymore."

"So it left you without a purpose?'

"Until I met you." Benny said and knew he better spend less time with his manager. He was an awful influence.

"Why didn't you ever tell me about her?" She purred.

"I hadn't really thought about her after I met you. Besides you always say everyone's conversations are just stolen from what we watch on TV. I didn't want you thinking what I feel isn't real." She went nuts when he got all sensitive like that. It wasn't fair. He knew she would go nuts, so that's why he said what he did, but he didn't want anyone going nuts for him but Kim. "Jenny, I've got to go."

"My Mom and sister aren't going to be home for hours. I thought maybe we could... fool around." She groped his biceps which had gotten considerably bigger since he started getting himself in shape for yo-yoing. A three-mile run everyday followed by pull-ups, push-ups, sit-ups, and two hours of bringing-yo-yo-ups.

"Jen, I can't. I've got to go pack. I'll call you from Chicago." He kissed her forehead which was what he always did to Kim, but that made more sense since Kim's forehead reached Benny's lips. Jen was a bit taller, so Benny had to stretch to make the kiss when they were both standing.

As he headed out the door Jen warned him, "Make sure you do call. I get real lonely going a day without you."

Benny hated himself for being such a phony. Jennifer was really cool, smart, pretty, fun to be with, and all around great, but any time she did anything to remind him she wasn't Kim, he wanted to get miles away from her.

Well, get her out of your mind. You're going to Chicago. The Windy City. The City of Big Shoulders. If you could make it there, you still might not be able to make it in New York. It was a town of high skyscrapers, deep dish pizzas, and mustached men.

The only other time Benny made it to this metropolis was in the ninth grade. He and Betty were members of the Future Business Leaders of America and they got to go on a three-day field trip to Chicago. They stayed in some run-down motel in the Southside by a convenience store that sold some of the naughty kids malt liquor. They visited the Sears Tower, the Museum of Science & Industry, and listened to a speech given by the CEO of Heinz Ketchup.

Benny knew this trip to Chicago was different as soon as he got out of the cab. Stan told Benny he had made reservations for a posh hotel two weeks in advance. Benny didn't know how fancy until the bellboys in their red uniforms insisted they be the ones to take his suitcase up to his room.

Benny had never felt like a VIP before. It made him a little nervous. After they checked into their rooms, Benny's phone rang. He wondered if it was a wrong number. Who knew how to reach him?

"How are you liking the life of luxury, Benny?" it was Stan. "I was thinking of heading down to the hotel lounge for some boozin' and cruisin', how would you like to join me?"

"That's a very tempting offer Stan, but I should probably, you know get some rest before the big day."

"You know what that sounds like to me?" Stan asked. Benny was worried it came across as rude and out of politeness he would need to join Stan, but then Mr. Friendly changed gears. "That sounds like a yo-yo champion. Get some beauty sleep and I'll see you bright and early in the morning."

Benny breathed a sigh of relief. Then he ate the mint left on his pillow and flipped around the dial on the television. And then he did get some beauty sleep.

And in the blackness he heard a voice. "You're a fraud. You ain't the real thing. You're nobody." Benny knew the voice was telling the truth, but he didn't want to confront it. He ran away. But the harder he ran, the louder the voice got. Then there was nowhere to run. A giant chasm was in front of Benny. It looked like a bottomless pit. Since the voice was getting nearer, Ben felt he had no choice. He jumped. But not far enough to make it across to the other side.

He fell for what felt like forever. When he realized the voice disappeared, Benny knew he made the right choice. Better to die than to have to face your failures. But then Benny stopped in mid-air and started spinning back up where he came from. He looked up and saw he was heading for a giant, outstretched hand with a string looped around its middle finger. Benny noticed the string was attached to his waist. And by then it was too late. He was in the hands of.... The Yo-Yo Kid? "You're nothing. Just a big phony. You're a...."

Ring. Ring. The phone woke Benny out of his nightmare. He put the receiver to his head and a silky, electronic voice said, "This is your wake-up call. It is currently 7:15. Good morning!" Benny hung up, rubbed his eyes, and rolled straight out of bed.

After a quick shower, there was a knock on the door. Benny opened up and saw Stan smiling like he had the greatest night of his life. Stan asked, "Did you have a good night's sleep?"

"No."

"Well get over it. You got a busy day ahead of you. You're scheduled for the preliminary round at 9:55 in the A.M.. I figure then you can check out the exhibits and what not. Just don't talk to anyone. I don't want your opponents psyching you out."

They headed down the hallway to the elevator and Benny went over the rules and regulations. In the preliminary round, the three judges, including last year's champ, asked you to do an array of yo-yo feats. If you didn't know a trick, you goofed up on a trick, or your form wasn't perfect, you were out. Only eight people made it out of this round. The lucky eight are then handed out a choreographed sequence. They had two hours to memorize and practice it. The two yo-yo masters who performed the sequence with the most skill made the finals. In the finals, anything went. Wow them. Zow them. Kapow them. Do whatever it took to get the first prize. Because both the first-place winner and the runner-up lost their amateur status since they both won prize money. The difference was the first-place winner got ten thousand dollars and their very own network TV special to showcase their talents. Second prize was one dollar.

Benny took a deep breath on the elevator ride down. When the door opened on the ground floor a large sign greeted them. "Yo-yo convention this-a-way." They followed the signs through the lobby past the hotel restaurant. Benny's stomach grumbled loudly so Stan promised, "I'll get you some breakfast later, but first let's get to the convention."

Stan Friendly needed to speak no more for they were there. It was a bit underwhelming. The whole convention was in a room no larger than Friendly Bank. There were tables set up by corporate sponsors giving away free yo-yos. Collectible yo-yos from yesteryear were being hawked by bearded men. Benny was disappointed that he was one of the youngest people there. He thought this convention was for kids, but everyone reeked of middle age, even though they were wearing adolescent t-shirts with corny slogans like "Yo-yo Adrian!". Stan and Benny walked past booths displaying instructional videos towards the back. They reached the closed double doors with a sign posting, "Quiet please, yo-yo competition in progress."

They began to walk through the door, but a hand stopped them. "You have to wait until the contestant has finished, sir. Let me see your contestant passes."

Stan and Benny dug into their pockets. They showed the burly guard their credentials and he told them to wait where they were. Stan gave these instructions to Benny, "I'm going to get us breakfast. I want you to watch your opponents. Spot their weaknesses. Especially Javier Hernandez at 9:05 and Edgar Jones at 9:40."

Stan walked away a few moments before security let Benny enter the room. There were eight or nine rows of metal chairs facing a tiny, temporary stage. Benny took note that there wouldn't be much room to maneuver.

The competition wasn't set up as a spectator's event, it didn't take long for Benny to get bored of the third-rate yo-yoers. Most of them were OK, but there was no panache to their presentation. He looked at his program to prevent going comatose. He recognized some names from the scouting reports Stan prepared. Javier Hernandez was last year's Cuban National Yo-Yo Champion. He defected last summer on a good will trip to Spain. He had never performed in the States, so no one knew what to expect or how he would adapt to American-style competition.

Then there was Edgar Jones, a physics student, who designed what he claimed to be "the perfect yo-yo". With it he attained the world record for the longest sleeper ever. Finally, there was Rebecca Monet, one of the few female contestants. She had won quite a few regional competitions but in "the boys club" of the yo-yo world she wasn't invited to the major tournaments. So, she used that to her advantage and started performing in a bikini. Most judges were now too busy drooling to recognize any flaws in her technique. She wasn't scheduled to go on until 10:05. Benny didn't know how he was going to last the next 40 minutes until he was allowed to enter the warm-up room.

Then with almost perfect timing Stan showed up with his food. Benny opened the bag to find a bagel and orange juice. Stan then started his running commentary. "This guy stinks. Don't freeze when you go up there like this guy did. Make sure to untangle your yo-yo before you go out there. This guy's not too bad, watch out for this Jimmy DuPont." Benny almost stood up to cheer when the middle judge read, "Jones, Harrison, Jackson, James, Humble, and Monet can now report to the warm-up room."

As Benny got up his overbearing manager reminded him, "Remember everything I told you the last few weeks."

Benny was one of six people to walk into the conference room, a.k.a. the warm-up room. Benny decided to keep to himself. Just concentrate on the yo-yo going up and down, up and down.

"Who are you?" asked a whiny voice. "I've never seen you at any of the competitions before."

Benny turned around to see a skinny guy wearing glasses, a crew cut, and a white lab coat, for some unknown reason. "My name's Benny James." Ben stuck out his hand to shake.

"I figured that was your name since it was the only contestant's name I didn't recognize. This isn't an open competition. How did you get invited if you haven't won any competitions before?"

"My man... uh..." Benny stopped himself when he realized that amateurs weren't allowed to have managers. "My man, my main man, Stan Friendly pulled some strings for me."

One of the judges entered the room and said, "Edgar Jones is on next." Benny's confrontational opponent walked out of the room but gave Benny the look meaning he better watch out.

Benny went back to his yo-yo, but a breathy, feminine voice tried comforting him. "Don't worry about him. Edgar's a big meanie. He used to try to intimidate me too"

From her voice Benny knew it had to be Rebecca Monet. What he didn't know was that she had already stripped down to her black bikini. After his eyeballs returned to his socket Benny pretended she was clothed normally. "That's the jerk who invented the perfect yo-yo?"

"Yep." She said while rubbing tropical oils all over her tanned belly.

Benny couldn't stop himself. He had to ask, "How can you go out there like that? Don't you have any self-respect? The judges aren't voting for your yo-yo skills."

She put her hand on his yo-yoing arm and asked, "You don't like what you see?"

He backed away and realized Stan was right. They were all a bunch of psyche out artists. Oh no, he didn't realize that yet. It wasn't until Rebecca whispered into his ear, "You don't have a chance in hell," and then walked away that Ben knew he was being picked on.

Benny hid back in his shell. If anyone else in the room talked, he would feign deafness. Just let the yo-yo move naturally. Up and down. "James. Benjamin James is on next." Ben took a deep breath. He breathed deeply a lot that day. Stan had told him it was good for the lungs. Benny walked out of the warm-up room on to the main stage. There was no spotlight and the lights weren't off, but Benny was still the center of attention.

He introduced himself to the crowd like he was back at Friendly Bank entertaining the nice people of Hatchet City. "Good afternoon everyone. I'm Benny James."

The bald judge on the left told him, "Yes, we know that. Let's see your sleeper. And let's see your rocking the cradle. And..."

The judges sang off a shopping list of tricks and Benny sleepwalked right through them. He thought this would be more of a challenge but making friends with his opponents was more difficult than jumping through the judges' hoops. While still on the stage Benny daydreamed about the final round where he would be able to do his thing. He would humiliate Edgar Jones and his perfect yo-yo. The loss would drive Edgar mad and Edgar would do anything to get back at Benny. Even kidnap Kim. Benny will save her though, like he always did. And then she would love him.

"Thank you, Ben. That was great." The judge to the right said. Ben walked off the stage to smatters of applause.

He sat back down next to Stan who stopped scribbling on his pad of paper to pat Ben's back and whisper, "You did great. The best one I've seen. Except for that geek with the glasses and lab coat."

Benny responded to that comment as though he was still feigning deafness. "I'm taking off Stan. I'll be back at noon when they announce the semi-finalists." As Benny got up he snuck a peek of what he assumed were Stan's notes about the contestants. Turned out Stan was just playing tic-tac-toe with himself.

As mentioned before, the convention was not going to make anyone's jaw drop. Benny was strolling around for one reason only. To find out what he could about Simon Wiesel, The Yo-Yo Kid. He went from booth to booth and here are some sample responses.

"Who?"

"Never heard of him."

"Yeah, I read about him. Some small town kid from Cutlet City or Hatchet City? I think it said he was going to be competing here."

Somehow in this haystack of ignorance, Benny found a needle of knowledge. A short man with the physique of an ice fisherman had heard of Simon Wiesel. "Yes, otherwise known as The Yo-Yo Kid."

"Do you know if he's still alive?"

"Goodness, I wouldn't know. I only saw his films. They're fun stuff. But I actually know someone who might know. You're going to be around for a while? Come back around two, I'll see if I can reach him."

Benny figured he earned the right to brag a little. "Yeah, I'll be around. I'm in the competition."

"Are you? Good for you. I actually won the amateur championship back in '72. It's a great stepping stone toward a career of professional yo-yoing."

After hearing this, Benny was not too confident about the prestige of this award any longer. Benny then returned to the yo-yo competition mere minutes before they announced who made it to the next round. Last year's winner Nester Noluch made the announcement. "Ladies and gentlemen, the judges, all three of us, have made our selections. In the top bracket the four semi-finalists are Chuck... and after I call your name please come up on stage. Chuck Bradley." Applause. "Javier Hernandez." Applause. "Shades McCoy." Applause. "Edgar Jones." Benny was the only one not clapping. "They will all be performing the choreographed sequence at 2:00. Now for the semi-finalists in the lower bracket...Rebecca Monet." Applause as she walked up with her tummy tucked in. "Benny James."

Benny jumped up and jogged on to the stage. Adoration still embarrassed him slightly, so Edgar Jones did Benny the favor of knocking him back to humble grounds, "You're going to get creamed rookie." Benny had no idea why Edgar continued playing the intimidation game. Chances were they wouldn't both make the finals.

As soon as they received their choreographed sequence Benny practically sprinted off the stage. Stan wanted to know where his investment was going. Benny gave him a vague answer then spent the next two hours in his hotel room practicing his routine while wishing Kim was there with him. She would know how Benny could get Edgar and all those other jerks to like him. Maybe if she was there Benny wouldn't even care what these other jerks thought of him.

Benny returned to the convention, several minutes before he needed to. He wanted to see if that former champ found out anything. Benny waited while the possible informant dealt with a customer. After selling a rare electric yo-yo that was discontinued because it occasionally surged electric shocks into the user's hand, the former champ turned his attention to Benny. "Can I help you with anything?"

"Yeah, did you find out anything about The Yo-Yo Kid?"

"Oh, right, right, right." He said remembering Benny's face. "My friend doesn't wish to divulge any information until he gets a better feel for who you are. His name's Jack Pratt. His phone number's on the piece of paper. Give him a call."

Jack Pratt? That was the phoniest name Benny had ever heard. This was all turning crazy and top secret. He felt pretty soon he would have to check if anyone was following him. Lost in thought, Benny missed the former champ's question the first time around. "How did you do in the competition, kid?"

Benny looked at his watch. "Oh man. I'm on in fifteen minutes." He ran off to his destiny.

Stan was angry as heck. "Where were you? You missed your warm-up."

Benny brushed him aside because this part of the contest would be a piece of cake unless the judges were sexist pigs and choose sleaze over skills. Soon as his name was called, Benny danced on to the stage. He spun with grace and dignity. The yo-yo became an extension of Benny James, it flowed and came back to him like true love. Behind the back, through the air, between his legs, suspended at a twenty-degree angle. He was the master and the audience respected it. They clapped like applause was going out of style. Benny waved to his admirers and walked meekly off the stage. He passed Rebecca Monet on the way to his seat. She blew him an arrogant, discreet little kiss.

No one else caught their little interaction, so Benny pretended it didn't happen as he seated himself next to Stan. Stan for once wasn't talking. His nerves were splattered. Rebecca didn't have half the control Ben did, but you could never underestimate the skin factor. She pulled out all the stops. Shaking her butt, bending over whenever possible, even doing a split while she did an around the world. The judge's scoreboards were undoubtedly soaked with drool. And when she ended her routine, all the yo-yo boys were chanting, "Rebecca, Rebecca, Rebecca."

The next two contestants were jokes. Either they had no business being there in the first place or Rebecca's performance completely robbed them of their motor skills. So Stan didn't say a word until the judges finished tabulating their final decision.

Nester Noluch walked back on stage. "Everyone, we've made our decision for the finalists of the Amateur World Yo-Yo Championships. From the top bracket we have a veteran. A three-time semifinalist here, but this is his first trip to the finals... Edgar Jones." Everyone clapped but Benny and the other semi-finalists. "From the lower bracket we have some young blood. This is his first appearance at the Championships and he's too ambitious to pay his dues...Benjamin James."

Stan couldn't believe it. He gave Benny the truest hug, he had ever given. "You did it." He screamed amidst the applause. Benny walked up to the stage which he had to share with his dreaded enemy.

Edgar stuck out his hand for Benny to shake. Benny obliged for the sake of the photographers of the yo-yo trade journals, but he wished he hadn't when Edgar whispered, "Like taking candy from a baby..."

Benny fought the urge to smack the skinny creep. He would show him soon enough. In three hours the finals would begin.

Saturday, February, 18, 1989
4:23 p.m.
Chapter Seven

Ever been so in love that the thought of being alone for another day is hell in a hand basket? That was how Benny James felt. He should have been on top of the world. He was a finalist to earn the crowning achievement in his profession along with a $10,000 check. He had a fifty-fifty chance. Benny should have been doing everything he could to improve those odds, but that numbness in his stomach wouldn't let him concentrate on anything but the cause of the numbing, Kim Feldman. He picked up the hotel phone and didn't give a second's thought to the hotel surcharges. But all he got was her answering machine.

"Hi, you've reached Kim and Rhonda. Neither of us are home right now, so why not leave a message?"

Benny seriously considered leaving a message, but then he hung up. Her voice was too much. Too much like heaven. He called back to hear the angel's trumpet.

"Hi, you've reached Kim and Rhonda. Neither of us are home right now, so why not leave a message?"

This time Benny followed her command. "Hi Kim… this is… um… Ben. I just wanted to hear your voice and I guess I did on the machine but… I'd like to hear it for real. I'm at the Yo-Yo Championships. I'm in the finals. That's what I do for a living now. I yo-yo. Um… I'll call you later."

He hung up and called back two more times to hear her voice. He figured after the competition she would have to love him. Because he would no longer be a latching, lovesick little schoolboy. He would be a winner. He was about to leave his hotel room to kick some tail downstairs, but he remembered another call he had to make.

"Hello," said an antiquated voice from long distance.

"I'd like to speak to Jack Pratt."

"Speaking."

"Um… My name's Ben James."

"And you're looking for Simon Wiesel. I know all about you. You're a yo-yoer. You're in the finals, eh?"

"Um… yeah. Do you yo-yo?"

"I've been known to. I'm just not one of those old codgers who likes associating with younger generations." Benny desperately wanted to ask Jack Pratt if he was Simon Wiesel. But before the thought translated into words, the old man answered, "No, Ben I'm not Simon Wiesel. I'm his authorized biographer. But I'll tell you everything you want to know about Simon on one condition."

"What do you want?"

"After you win the competition, in your victory speech you need to tell everyone, 'Simon Wiesel would be ashamed of you.'"

Benny had more questions than he had for his professors in four years of higher education. He started with, "How do you know I'm going to win?"

"How do I know? You're the Yo-Yo Kid. That's how I know." Jack Pratt hung up the phone. Benny tried calling again. He figured they were accidentally disconnected. He didn't realize the old man was trying to be cryptic. But Benny got no further contact, not even an answering machine.

Benny returned to the convention floor. Things were winding down. All the dealers were packing away their products. Benny looked for that former champ who gave him Jack Pratt's phone number, but his table was long gone. Everyone was hyped about the finals, to see what the greatest young minds in the yo-yo universe could do with themselves. There was a rumor that Edgar Jones might attempt to break his own record of world's longest sleeper.

Benny wasn't hyped. He was too busy being shocked when he saw Stan with his arm wrapped around Rebecca Monet. Benny was disgusted with that filthy traitor for associating with the enemy.

Stan charmed him though like he always could, "Ben. Benny. Benny. Ben. I want you to meet Rebecca."

"We already met." Although not when she was fully clothed as she was presently.

"Stan's going to represent me now," she said with such a happy smile on her face.

"Oh… that's just great."

"Hey Ben, those were just head games I was playing with you before. I'm rooting for you against that creep Edgar."

"Oh OK." Benny said after seeing she wanted to make nice. "It's just you shouldn't mess with people's heads like that. It's not right."

Stan put his free arm on Benny's shoulder and told Rebecca, "See, didn't I tell you he was a great kid. Now go practice, so you can knock us dead."

Benny knew when he wasn't wanted. Let Stan seduce the young harlot, someone's got to entertain the masses. Benny stretched out because he was going to have to be limber by showtime. He touched his toes. Stretched his legs. Extended his elbows.

"This isn't a track meet, rookie." said that whiny voice.

Benny saw it was his rival looking for trouble again. Benny remembered his Mom's favorite saying. If you have nothing nice to say, shut your big mouth. So Benny continued loosening his muscles as Edgar Jones ragged on him. "You're no match for me and my yo-yo. You're going to get your butt handed to you. You're…"

Edgar stopped in mid-sentence because Benny had enough. He put on his yo-yo and wrapped it around Edgar's neck. If Benny pulled his finger a little harder Edgar would have choked. Benny warned him, "Don't mess with The Yo-Yo Kid." The yo-yo wound back to Benny's hand and Benny walked away from his obnoxious opponent.

As soon as Edgar stopped gasping for air he threatened Benny, "If I tell the judges what you just did, you'll be disqualified."

Benny gave him a look. "Then you shouldn't tell anyone."

Edgar wouldn't tell anyone. Soon as anyone ever stood up to his bullying, he always cowered away. It happened when he was nine and his little sister was sick of him throwing her underwear outside the house. She punched him in the gut and he never bothered her again. It happened when his neighbor's dog bit his leg after years of mock meowing. And it happened today with Benny James. Edgar stood as far from Benny as the close quarters of the competition would allow after that confrontation.

Edgar had to go first and even though his nerves were still frazzled he showed what science could do for the yo-yo. Aerodynamics, laws of motion, all served their purpose as Edgar broke his previous record for longest sleeper ever recorded. He did a whole array of tricks to which the crowd gooed and gahhed, but there was no artistry so first place was Benny's to lose.

When Benny's name was called, it was the audience that almost lost it. Everyone laughed at Benny in his dress shirt, slacks, bow tie, and Lone Ranger mask. Benny was now officially The Yo-Yo Kid and he was not getting any respect, but that didn't stop him from putting on the show of the year. With his left hand he flicked a yo-yo toward the crowd and did a textbook perfect around-the-world. The unexpected was what came out of his right hand, two yo-yo's yo-yoing. Then he created the illusion that he was juggling the three yo-yos by flicking them in the air and letting them come back to his hands in alternating order. Applause spread like wildfire. Benny then let a yo-yo from each hand tangle together and he started jumping rope. Somehow the yo-yos never stopped spinning. Greatness was in the air and everyone was breathing it in. They were all pumped for a majestic finale. What in heaven's name was going to end it all? Benny topped everyone's dreams by stealing a trick from the original Yo-Yo Kid. He threw the yo-yo toward the ceiling and wrapped it around a hanging light fixture. He swung himself into the crowd and the yo-yo spun back to his hand. The crowd clapped and roared louder than they would have at a knockout by Muhammad Ali or a final bow by Laurence Olivier or if they were present when Shakespeare scribbled The End to Hamlet. It was madness and beauty and everyone thanked the Gods that they were present for perfection. Benny bowed a couple times and noticed a flower was thrown to his feet. It was a yellow rose. He picked it up and smelled the rose which only served to remind him of what he was missing.

He wasn't missing Stan Friendly putting his arm around him saying, "I knew you had it in you kid. Suck it in. This could be the greatest moment of your life."

The crowd started chanting, "Benny, Benny, Benny, BEN-NEE!"

But this was nothing. This was vain happiness. Benny had experienced true happiness and he wanted more of it. He sat down next to Stan forcing Rebecca to stand while the judges conferred and the crowds sang, "BEN-NEE! BEN-NEE! BEN-NEE!"

This could have been too much for a young man's ego. Fortunately Benny had Stan to keep his feet on the ground. Stan handed the star a deck of 3x5 index cards and commanded, "When you go up there I want you to read this."

"I can't Stan I…"

"Listen kid, don't tell me you can't. Have I ever been wrong? Go up there and read it. That's your victory speech. They'll love you for it."

Benny only had a minute to wonder which of the three stooges he most closely resembled until the judges walked up on stage to announce, "Ladies and gentlemen, by unanimous and overwhelming support we have our Amateur World Yo-Yo Champion. I can't remember ever being as excited by the prospects of the future of yo-yoing as I am right now. I am pleased to announce our new champ… Benjamin James."

Ben walked down the aisle to the sound of his name being roared. Stan ripped Benny's mask off as he got close to the stairs so everyone could see what a clean-cut young man he was. Benny shook the judges' callused hands, folded the check into his pocket, and lifted the heavy golden trophy in the shape of a yo-yo for everyone to see.

Last year's winner Nester Noluch was still holding the microphone, but the roar of the crowd dulled his voice. "Ben, I know better than anyone what an honor it is to be crowned world champ. Is there anything you would like to say to your fans?"

"Thank you. sir." Benny took the microphone. He looked out at the small crowd. He then looked at the speech Stan wrote for him. From the first line of "Who says yo-yos are for nerds?" Benny knew Stan's speech wasn't right for this moment, so he said what felt true. "Simon

Wiesel would be ashamed of you." That was the second record broken at that year's Amateur World Yo-Yo Championship and Convention. Longest sleeper ever recorded and quickest a roaring crowd was stunned into silence.

Friday, February 24, 1989
5:30 p.m.
Chapter Eight

"But you just got home! You're already packing again?"

"Yeah Dad." Benny said as he looked for another clean pair of socks. He found a black pair in the back of his underwear drawer.

"Does Stan have a job lined up for you? He didn't mention anything to me at work."

"Yeah, next month I'm going to California to film a segment for a TV show called *Golly, Gee Whiz*. But I'm going to Arizona now. Jimmy's coming with me too during his Spring Break. I asked Mom, she said it was alright."

"Arizona… Jeez. I mean what…" Henry James noticed his son was concentrating more on making sure his clothes fit in his suitcase than on his father. "You know Benny, Stan's very upset with your victory speech. He said you offended a lot of people. If you did what he asked he said you would have gotten a lot of endorsement money."

"Sorry, Dad."

"Sorry? Benny, I mean you know people like myself, your mother, Stan. We work hard for your benefit. It would be nice if you listen to us once in a while and show some appreciation."

Benny stopped packing and put on his worn down hiking boots. He wondered how Stan became his third parent. "Thanks, Dad. I love you and I appreciate your hard work." He gave his Dad a hug and ran his suitcase out of the house.

Henry wondered when he stopped mattering all together. His daughter exiled herself to Siberia, now his sons preferred other old men to his company? The despair was so evident on his face that when he went downstairs to watch some TV Jimmy asked, "Jeez Dad. What's got your underwear tied in a knot?"

"Go to your room Jim." Jimmy cursed under his breath as he did what he was told, until the father realized his younger son could be of use. "Wait Jim, I want to talk to you. Why are you going to Arizona?"

"There's some old yo-yo master Benny wants to learn from."

"Then why are you going?" Dad asked.

"Benny doesn't want to spend a week alone with an old man."

"Oh." Henry James said as he feared for his future. Is this what old age had in store for him? No one willing to spend time with you except for your friends on the TV.

Benny wasn't thinking too much about the future as he drove Stan Friendly's Mustang to Pretty Boy Floyd's Bar and Grill. There were only a couple cars in the dusty parking lot. It was still daytime, so not too many people were starting their liquor injections. As our hero walked into the empty saloon Jennifer was behind the bar with her nose in a paperback book. As Benny got closer he still couldn't read the title.

"Hi," he smiled crookedly.

Her first instinct was to smile right back at his goofball grin, but then she remembered how angry she was with him. With a temperature of absolute zero she asked, "What do you want to drink?"

"Jen, I'm sorry I didn't call you from Chicago. I had the competition to worry about, but I won and..."

"What do you want to drink?" she asked with a hint of dementia in her eyes.

"You." Benny joked as he tried to plant a smooch on her. Then without warning she grabbed a bottle of beer from the refrigerator and hurled it at him. By the good grace of God it didn't break as it smacked Benny's shin, but it hurt like nobody's business.

He screamed ow as he limped toward her. He hopped over the bar and wrapped his arms around her, so she couldn't cause any more pain. "Let go." She screamed.

The big, hulking, bearded bouncer ran over there and asked, "Jen, is this dweeb bothering you?"

"No, I'm not bothering her. It's just a boyfriend/girlfriend fight." Benny said as he let go of her.

"You better step away from her or this will be a two-hit fight. I'll hit you. You'll hit the ground."

Benny couldn't believe the steroid freak said that. He hadn't heard that since the seventh grade. "Jennifer, can you tell this guy to leave while we talk?"

"I think you should leave Ben."

The big guy was praying he could inflict some pain. "You heard her, nerd." The bouncer cracked his knuckles for emphasis.

"Alright. Alright. I'm leaving town for a week Jen, so I guess we'll talk when I get back." He kissed her forehead and she pushed him away. The bouncer had enough, he picked Ben up by his shirt collar and pushed him outside.

So Benny's intentions for visiting Pretty Boy Floyd's went completely unfulfilled. He wanted to tell Jennifer that he was still in love with Kim and was going to try to see her on the way to Arizona. But to make matters worse he now suddenly had some passion for this wild child, Jennifer Royce.

Sunday, February 26, 1989
5:21 a.m.
Chapter Nine

The drive was long and it was hard. Benny made sure to thank
Stan profusely for lending him his convertible. Benny knew he gave Stan
twenty percent of his prize money, even though his Dad told him a
manager was only supposed to get fifteen, but he was still touched by
the trust Stan showed by handing over the keys to his Ford Mustang.
Right now Jimmy was driving 90 straight into the sunset. Benny was too
upset to drive. Earlier they took a detour to try to reunite true love.
Benny went back to his alma mater to remind Kim how much he loved
her only to find out she was on Spring Break. He would now have to
wait until next Sunday on the way back home from Jack Pratt's house.
He flicked his yo-yo up at the sky as the stars appeared one by one.

The desert was beautiful. Benny was too distracted to truly
appreciate it, even if it was just like he imagined. Plenty of nothing,
mountains in the background, an occasional two armed cactus, and
coyotes howling in the air. After a while the dryness hurt Benny's lips.
He licked them because it seemed an obvious way to resolve the
chapness, but that only made things worse.

Eventually Benny licked himself to sleep. He curled against the
door, dreaming that it was daylight and it was a showdown at the old,
western Ghost Town. On the other side of the dusty road was The Yo-Yo
Kid. His mask was on, so was his cape and long underwear. He yelled to
Ben, "Draw, varmint. I said to draw."

Benny reached for his holster. He drew his yo-yos and sprung
them at The Yo-Yo Kid only to discover they didn't have enough reach.
By this time The Yo-Yo Kid was already shooting his guns and his
mouth. "You yellow bellied phony. There's only one Yo-Yo Kid and you
ain't him."

The bullets hit Benny and as he bled to death he noticed all the
townspeople were different versions of Kim. Jennifer was there because

she was the taller, crasser version of Kim. So why couldn't Benny love her? Especially since she was the only one to rush to his side. "Ben. Benny. Benny." Her only flaw was she spoke in Jimmy's crackling voice.

"Benny. Wake up big bro. I need money." Benny awakened to the bright fluorescent lights of a gas station in the middle of nowhere.

Ben asked, "How much further?"

"I figure four or five hours. Unless a UFO picks us up."

Ben sneered at his little brother. There he went picking at old scabs. Just because Ben said he was a little nervous about the Southwest because that's where all the alien abductions took place, Jimmy wouldn't stop teasing him.

After they filled up the gas tank. Ben took his turn at taking his time driving. After Jimmy fell asleep Ben remembered the phone call he got in his hotel room immediately after winning the Amateur World Yo-Yo Championships.

"Congratulations Ben."

"Who is this?" Ben didn't think anyone had his hotel room phone number besides Stan and this certainly wasn't Stan's voice.

"Ben this is Jack Pratt. Congratulations. I told you, you'd win."

"You did sir, and I told them all Simon Wiesel would be ashamed of them."

The old man laughed for a good long time. "Heh heh. He would be. So I guess you want to learn a thing or two, huh?"

"Yeah, like why did you want me to say Simon Wiesel was ashamed of them?"

Jack Pratt was silent. Benny wasn't sure if he hung up on him again, but then the shaky voice spoke. "A bald man and a redheaded guy got to you didn't they?"

Benny racked his brain. "No. Oh yeah, they were the judges. They really ran up there and cut my speech short after I said what you wanted."

"Those old coots started the Amateur Championships with me back in the sixties. It was a way to honor the old-time yo-yo men like Simon Wiesel and to pass those values on to young yo-yoers, but those old creeps decided they would aim for profits instead of utopia. Simon Wiesel would be ashamed. You got any other questions?"

"Yeah about The Yo-Yo Kid, did he..."

"You are The Yo-Yo Kid Ben, don't forget that. But I got other things to tell you. Now that you're rich, you can afford to make it out to Arizona on your own. You can stay with me. I won't bill you too much for a room. Heh heh heh."

That was when Benny got a little suspicious of the old man's motives so he asked, "Is it OK if I bring my little brother along too?"

"Sure. But what makes you think I won't kill him too? Just kidding kid. Heh heh heh. I'll send you directions in the mail."

So Benny brought his little brother to the desert for some wisdom and to remind him there was a whole great, wonderful, whacky world outside Hatchet City. Away from television screens and bored teens, there were yo-yo kings and lovely queens.

The sun was peeking over the horizon when Benny noticed he was only a few miles from Jack Pratt's address. It was not right to show up at that early hour, so he pulled the car over to a rest area, got in the tiny backseat and caught a few Zzzzzzzs. There were no more dreams because Benny tossed and turned more than he actually slept. When the sun told him it was officially a decent hour, he pulled back into the front seat and drove away. Jimmy slept as they followed the final steps to Jack Pratt's directions. They passed a giant sign reading, "Flying Meadow, a planned community". One street led to another and they were there. 24 straight hours of driving had brought them to Jack Pratt's driveway.

All the architecture in Jack Pratt's neighborhood had a rock motif. Everything was painted in shades of brown and dark reds. Jack Pratt's house was no different. It looked like a giant boulder with doors and windows. There was a rock garden in the front yard since apparently there was not enough water in the desert for a plant garden.

Jimmy wanted to stay in the car as Benny went to knock on the door. After a long wait the door opened meekly. A hunched over man with a slight resemblance to Albert Einstein must be Jack Pratt.

"Mr. Pratt?" Benny asked nervously.

"Mr. Kid? Mr. Yo-Yo Kid, come on in. You didn't bring any bags?"

Benny told him, "They're in the car with my brother, sir."

"Well bring them in with your brother." The old man walked inside with the help of a wooden cane. Without it gravity could be too much for him.

Benny went out to the car to grab his sack of clothes. Jimmy immediately asked, "So is he going to kill us?"

"No. He's a good old man, a good senior citizen. He's going to teach me a lot, I can tell." Benny said trying more to convince himself than his baby brother.

They walked inside the house. It had the stench of affluence and old age. There was a giant TV, a pool in the back, and a guest bedroom where Jack Pratt was waiting for the brothers. "Here's your room." There was only one bed which made both brothers nervous. They were going to have to sleep together.

"This is quite a nice house, Mr. Pratt."

"Yeah, yeah. With money you can buy things. You boys want anything to eat? I've got some mayonnaise sandwiches I made last night."

"Oh… uh… no thanks sir. We ate breakfast before coming here." Benny lied through his teeth. He was having doubts about the usefulness this old man could provide.

"Well, put your things away and then meet me outside by the pool. We'll talk."

After taking forever to get away from hearing distance Jimmy told his older brother, "This guy creeps me out. Tell him I didn't get any sleep last night or make up some other excuse… I'm staying away."

Benny urged his brother to come along, but to no avail. Jimmy told his older brother as he walked out the room, "Hey, if he tries anything funny, just scream and I'll beat him up for you."

Benny laughed nervously as he walked to the backyard. He put his hand in his pocket and gripped his yo-yo. If the old man did try anything funny, he would pop him in the head. Benny opened the sliding glass door to get out of the air conditioning and into the morning desert heat. The old man was sitting in a deck chair with his feet dangling in the pool. Ben sat next to him but kept his feet dry.

"I've been waiting for you for a long time."

"Sorry, Mr. Pratt we could have been here a couple hours earlier, but I didn't want to wake you up."

"Heh heh heh." When Mr. Pratt laughed his mustache quivered. "A couple hours don't matter. I've been waiting for years… decades for a successor. "Benny knew it! He knew this old man was Simon Wiesel, but why did he pretend he was Jack Pratt? Benny stopped wondering because he couldn't think and listen at the same time. "My children… they're all morons. My grandchildren too. I tried to teach a couple of yo-yo champs in the '60's and '70's, that's why we started the yo-yo competition. To find young blood. But the champs were never the type of people I need. They were all greedy and… well, it never worked out. But I have a feeling about you."

"So you are Simon Wiesel? You are The Yo-Yo Kid."

"No. I told you, Simon Wiesel is dead. And you're The Yo-Yo Kid. I'm Jack Pratt."

Benny wondered what this old guy could teach him then. But he didn't ask because the old guy was going to answer him any way. "But you want to know about Simon Wiesel and you want to know about me and what good an old fart like me can do for a hot shot like you?"

"Yeah, I guess."

Jack Pratt smiled because he didn't get a captive audience too often. His wife and friends were mostly all dead. His kids hated him and were counting the days until they collected his inheritance. His neighbors berated him for constantly complaining, so he made himself comfortable and began talking as though he rehearsed this story a hundred thousand times. "It's funny how our lives aren't like in the movies. It doesn't all make up one story. One part of your life has nothing to do with another. Then when you try to retell a life, you forget parts of it and you lose track of whether something you remember actually happened or if you just saw it on TV. But we'll try to make sense out of a life.

"Simon Wiesel was born to Romanian Jews. In case you don't know, Jews have a long history of being kicked out of their homes. For Simon Wiesel's parents it was no different. They fled Romania on a boat to New York City so they could raise Simon and his three sisters on streets paved with gold. Things were not as great as they had hoped. Simon's mother and father had to work hard and so did the children once they were big enough to work in the garment business. Long hours and abusive supervisors made Simon yearn for something else. When a traveling circus came to town, 12-year-old Simon Wiesel stowed away with them. Instead of learning arithmetic and social studies, Simon learned how to shoot himself out of a cannon and how to tame wild lions. He earned his keep selling peanuts, but he considered that part of his apprenticeship until he was ready to step into the three rings. Simon just didn't know what trade to learn. Everybody loves clowns, so Simon tried that, but offstage all the clowns were mean drunks that no one wanted to associate with. The Flying Flasgovs wanted to teach their fellow Romanian the art of trapeze, but Simon didn't have faith in other people's competence when his life was on the line. Then a new act joined the troupe. A marksman who with a bow and arrow could slice an apple in half from fifty yards away. Igor The Incredible was his name. The ringmaster forced Igor to wear a Robin Hood costume and Igor's act was to only consist of tricks with the bow and arrow, but Igor could make anything into a weapon. Once in a game of cards, the clowns caught Igor with a king up his sleeve. They would have torn him apart, but Igor flicked one card after another into the clown's foreheads, knocking them all unconscious. And these were big clowns, let me tell you. It sounds impossible, but Igor understood force, momentum, and all of those other fancy physics words. To an impressionable youth, this man appeared to be the toughest man alive. So one day Simon asked Igor if he could use an assistant. Igor was not willing to teach anyone everything he knows about the physical world for it might be turned against him one day. But he would help Simon master one object and one object only. After a long night of thinking Simon decided the yo-yo would be his trade. Igor laughed for a few minutes when he was shown what a yo-yo was. He put it on his finger and could not figure it out, but he told Simon to leave him and come back in the morning. The next day Simon came to Igor's trailer to see him throwing knives with the yo-yo, swinging from tree branches with the yo-yo. These are tricks you can do Ben, but it took Igor one night to harness the skills it took you years to master.

"Igor taught Simon what could be done with the yo-yo and soon Igor The Incredible had a sidekick, The Yo-Yo Kid. Simon wore a bank robber mask, a yellow shirt with a red Y sewn on the back of a cape and Igor the Incredible and The Yo-Yo Kid became the star attraction at the Hotchky Brothers Circus. For two grand years The Yo-Yo Kid and Igor The Incredible amazed audiences around America, but disaster struck. Ever hear of the great circus fire of 1926? Rumor has it one of the Hotchky Brothers set the tent on fire to collect the insurance money, but he would have had to be one heartless son of a gun to do that. All the animals died. Fifteen audience members and 23 and a half members of the circus family."

"Twenty-three and a half?" Benny broke into the monologue.

"Yes, that's what the newspapers said. The half was Tiny Teresa, a midget. Anything to sell a paper, huh? But more important for this story was that Igor The Incredible died. Leaving The Yo-Yo Kid without a home, without a job, without a family, and without a mentor. He had no choice but to return to his family in New York City. He hopped trains and hitchhiked from town to town. Along the way a small town in the Catskills captured Simon. He learned of a vaudeville show searching for performers..."

"Wait... wait... Mr. Pratt, how do you know all this?" Benny asked his elder.

Jack Pratt looked at the kid and decided enough with the facades. "Do you want to know the truth or do you want to hear the story I was going to tell you?"

"The truth."

"You're sure? I had a good story." Jack Pratt knew Benny was dead set on reality. "Alright. I'll tell you how I know all this, but let me finish talking about Simon. He tried out for a vaudeville show run by a cruel monster. His name was Lenny Friendly and his existence gave me faith that there is a devil. People were nothing to him. All that mattered were money and power. When Lenny saw Simon's skills with the yo-yo he offered him the world. He would have a new home, new job, new family, if he would sign some papers and perform for Lenny Friendly. Simon knew no better. All he knew was the seemingly impossible.

"People came from miles away to see him swing on to a stage and make a pastrami sandwich with his yo-yos instead of his hands. Lenny knew he had a star. He marketed him as the main attraction for all the girls to see. They traveled around the country, but instead of small town fairgrounds Simon was playing theatres and operahouses. Oh yes, at first they played flophouses but the theaters had to get bigger since they couldn't contain enough paying suckers. Two a days. Three a days. The yo-yo never left Simon's finger. He'd perform for a crowd of a thousand or for one lonely orphan. The money didn't matter, he loved the adoration. He could be seductive when he was holding his yo-yo and he seduced Hollywood. The studios lined up for miles to put him in their pictures. The highest bidder probably won, but Simon never saw any of the money. He didn't mind though since he was seeing more money than he ever thought existed. And he was seeing girls. In Hollywood even the girls who weren't pretty enough for the screen... oy they were too pretty. It was a different world. For once Simon was being pampered but he was too restless a kid to stay in his dressing room waiting and waiting between scenes. So he would go on long walks around the studio lot and around the neighborhood with his yo-yo. One late night, as he was swinging around the neighborhood, he heard screams of, 'No... don't. I'll bring you the money tomorrow. I promise.' A little, bitty man was being threatened by big goons with metal pipes. Then the spirit of Igor the Incredible took control of Simon. The Yo-Yo Kid turned the corner and flung his yo-yos into the two goons' foreheads. He knocked one of them out cold, but the other guy dodged the yo-yo. He swung his pipe at Simon, but with his spare yo-yo Simon swiped the metal pipe out of the thug's hands. The criminal knew he was no match for The Yo-Yo Kid without a weapon so he ran home to Mama. Benjamin, you should have seen the look on the little man's face. It was awe. It was more than the adoration Simon ever saw on stage as an entertainer. This was more of a dependence. The little man knew he would not be alive if it wasn't for The Yo-Yo Kid. Simon loved that feeling he got from helping people.

"So by day he was Simon Wiesel, The Yo-Yo Kid, the movie star. By night, he was The Yo-Yo Kid, hero. He patrolled the worst areas of Los Angeles looking for trouble. When his movies came out it wasn't hard for criminals and victims to identify the vigilante as The Yo-Yo Kid. The newspapers loved it. The women loved it. Simon loved it. But let us get back to the women. Simon was the most desirable bachelor, this side of Casanova. Not only was he a movie star, but he was a hero. He had his choice of any woman he wanted, but he only wanted one. A married one. Married to Lenny Friendly, no less, but he couldn't keep his hands off her. She was a Southern Belle. Blonde, blonde hair, a twang to her voice and it wasn't that long, OK, it took Lenny four years to find the lovers with their arms around each other. Lenny cursed Simon and promised him he would never work in Hollywood again. And he was right. Because of contracts and lawsuits, no one in show business could afford to work with Simon. But Simon didn't care. His heart was in his night job. Fighting crime with his mask and cape and sneaking around during the day, into the bedroom of Joanne Friendly. Simon got the last laugh. Lenny's two children, belong to him in name only."

Benny had a question, "So did you run off with Joanne and your kids?"

"Ah, you're a romantic, aren't you Benjamin? No, Joanne enjoyed Lenny's money too much, and unless Simon turned to crime, he couldn't afford a family. He liked being a hero too much. Besides it was too risky to stop their love from being forbidden. If Joanne got a divorce and they were allowed to love each other in public, the passion might have disappeared as quickly as Simon's savings disappeared. Not too quickly. It took maybe two years. Yes, it must have been two years, it was 1933. America was in the middle of a Great Depression. Work was hard to come by and Simon was too honest a man to turn his yo-yos to crime. He went from movie studio to movie studio, but no one would touch him. So he took the only job he could get, security at the docks. It was still widely known around town that Simon was beating up crooks and goons, so the dockmaster knew the docks would be safe. No one did mess with the docks, it was easy money until the longshoremen went on strike. The dockmaster convinced Simon they were all lazy bums manipulated by the mob. They were right that the union was run by mobsters, but most of the fellows on strike were hard workers who wanted more compensation. But Simon and some other hired muscle were paid to beat the heck out of the picketers. A lot of the longshoremen were strong, stubborn types. They weren't scared easily, so Simon had to use excessive force and killed one of the workers. He was so ashamed and guilty. He quit his job, he quit seeing Joanne, and spent his days wondering how he could live with himself. He decided to throw away his yo-yo..."

"And that's how you became Jack Pratt?" Benny asked impatiently.

"No. No. No. Simon is Simon and Jack is Jack. Simon gave up his yo-yo. He worked on farms across California. Where there was work there was Simon. Then there was that big day in December 1941. The Japanese bombed Pearl Harbor and America was at war. Uncle Sam needed all the warriors he could get. So a man in army green showed up one day at an orange grove in Bakersfield, California. America needed Simon to lead a secret yo-yo task force. Simon told them his yo-yo days were behind him, but they threatened him with jail time for his earlier days of illegal crime fighting. So Simon agreed to teach a select crew of four men, everything Igor The Incredible taught him years before. And that's how Simon Wiesel met Jack Pratt."

"Who are you Mr. Pratt?"

Jack Pratt wasn't just talking to Benny anymore. He was speaking to everyone who ever asked him that question. His dead wife, his kids, his lawyers. Only thing was Benny James was the only listener present for this revelation. "Jack Pratt was a freelance writer hired by Life magazine to write about the soon to be famous Yo-Yo Brigade. The magazine figured it would make for a good reader friendly story about unique soldiers. So they sent Jack Pratt, a young bachelor who lived for nothing but adventure. One night Jack and Simon shared a few drinks and a few stories. Jack was awfully wealthy. He inherited a lot of money so he wrote just to kill time. The paychecks didn't matter to him. Jack and Simon grew to like each other. Then one night Base 236, the base where the Yo-Yo Brigade was stationed, was bombed. Everyone in the Yo-Yo Brigade, but Simon Wiesel was killed. He was taking a crap at the time. The luckiest crap in the history of war. He came back to see his four fellow brigadiers and Jack Pratt all a bloody mess. But Simon wasn't the type of guy to let an opportunity go to waste. He switched his dog tag with Pratt's, and as far as the US Army was concerned, Simon Wiesel, blacklisted yo-yo master was dead."

"So you are Simon Wiesel? You are the Yo-Yo Kid?"

"No you shmendrick. We went through this already. I'm Jack Pratt. Simon Wiesel is dead. I came back to the US. The army decided to put the kibosh on the Yo-Yo Brigade story since it would have only been demoralizing to the country. So as Jack Pratt I now didn't have any responsibilities as a journalist. I didn't have a family, no lovers, as far as I knew. I didn't have any friends, all I had was tons of money. So I opened a delicatessen. Got married. Had kids. They had kids and you're the first person I ever told this story to."

"I don't believe it." Benny said.

"Yes, it's quite a life I've lived."

"No. I mean I don't believe your story sir. It's like a mixture of every movie I've ever seen."

"As far as I know Benjamin, it's the truth. Maybe I have gone senile and I've confused my life with what I've seen on TV. I don't have any way to prove my story. All of Simon Wiesel's youthful possessions are long gone. I suppose I could have made up any of it. Maybe it's all a lie and I've believed it for long enough that it's truth."

Benny pulled out his wooden yo-yo. "Here's how you can prove it."

Jack Pratt or Simon Wiesel or The Yo-Yo Kid or whoever he was took the yo-yo. He put the string around his finger. "It's been so many years. I don't know if my arthritis can take it." He didn't get out of his chair. The old man knew he couldn't stand and yo-yo at the same time anymore. He let the yo-yo dangle and then spun it back up. "Well, it's not exactly like riding a bicycle." He said but with every spin you could see the improvement. Benny felt like he was watching the great Louie

Armstrong rediscovering his trumpet in heaven. "This is the water fountain. Open your mouth Benjamin." Ben did as he was told and Jack spun the yo-yo against the pool's water, so it spouted directly into Ben's mouth. "How many things in life have you done just for the memory?" Jack asked as Ben spat out the chlorinated water. "Memories don't last forever, you know."

"Is that why you called me out here Mr. Pratt? To teach me that?"

"No. That's not why Benjamin. I had an idea. I've tried it before, but you're the only one who's seemed right. Tell me, why do you live? What do you want out of life?"

Benny didn't say her name. He just said what she represented. "Love."

"So you are a romantic? What are you going to live for after you've been with her for a year?"

"I'll live for her."

"Alright, how about after two years? What I'm trying to get at is I've been in love and it always fades away. Doubt me all you want."

"What should I live for then?" Benny said while doubting all he wanted.

"For your fellow human being. I'm talking about doing good for this world. I watch TV. I see all the gangs and drugs on the city streets. The world needs a new Yo-Yo Kid to clean this mess up. Trust me, there's no better feeling than saving a man's life."

"And you think I can do it?"

"No, I want you to recommend someone."

"Oh," Benny said with a tinge of rejection. But he couldn't get too down because before he knew it a yo-yo spun out of Mr. Pratt's hand and thwacked him in the head.

"Of course, I think you can do it, you moron. Get out of here before I change my mind completely. And leave that yo-yo with me."

Benny walked into his quarters. He was glad to get out of the desert sun anyway. It was getting too hot for his pale skin. Jimmy was lying in bed reading a magazine. "Benny, we've got to get out of here. This guy subscribes to Circus Weekly. He's a nut." He tossed the glossy magazine to Benny. Benny flipped through the magazine glancing at articles titled, "Which tightrope is the tightest?", "How to fit more clowns in your car", and a pin-up of the ringmaster of the month. Jimmy asked his older brother, "How crazy is this guy?"

Benny put down the magazine. "Pretty crazy. He tells so many bad jokes and he lies so much you don't know what's true."

"What does he want from you?" Jimmy asked.

"He wants me to be a hero."

Friday, March 3, 1989
6:01 a.m.
Chapter Ten

Twenty million yo-yos were coming his way from every direction. It was so claustrophobic that it had to be a dream. When Benny finally woke up he sighed with relief. He then went into the kitchen to eat some breakfast. It was going to be a long, hard day of training, so Benny stuck the two biggest slices of bread into the toaster oven. He went into the refrigerator to get some jam, but twenty yo-yos zipped at him. Instead of toast yo-yos popped out of the toaster. Yo-yos were coming out of the freezer, from the pantry, everywhere. And then there was that voice, "Only a real Yo-Yo Kid can play with yo-yos."

"Up and at 'em, boys." Jack Pratt's voice boomed into the bedroom. Benny rubbed the cold sweat off his face. It was just another silly dream within a dream. It was time for day two of his training. It was still dark outside which made sense since the clock read 5:30. Not even the early bird was awake.

Benny shook his brother, "Come on Jimmy, you said you wanted in on the training too."

Jimmy could barely get out of bed. Their previous day of training was too exhausting. A six-mile run followed by ten minutes of sit-ups. Three hundred push-ups. Ten minutes of jumping rope. Then they spent the next hour with the yo-yo. Mayonnaise sandwiches for lunch. Then six more hours of yo-yoing. Jimmy didn't think he could take another minute of it, but Benny had to beg and plead Jack Pratt to let his brother in on the secrets of the yo-yo. So Jimmy had no choice but to get up and further his education.

Soon as it looked like Jimmy was alive, Benny left the room for breakfast. He looked everywhere to make sure this wasn't another dream where yo-yos might be lurking behind every corner. But then one smacked him in the stomach. "Owww." He screamed. It hurt like a dickens and the pain wasn't waking him up.

"Didn't I tell you, always keep your stomach flexed!"

Benny whined, "I just woke up."

"Thieves and criminals won't hesitate to sucker punch your gut even if you just woke up, you big baby."

"You're crazy." Benny screamed as he poured himself some oat bran cereal.

"Crazy like a fox. Right? That's what you mean, crazy like a fox."

"Sure. Whatever. Yeah, you're crazy like a fox." Momentarily Benny wished he never came here and instead was lying on the grass with Kim looking at clouds shaped like elephants. But right now Benny wouldn't mind sharing that patch of grass with Jenny either. But Benny grew content with his present location when Jimmy walked into the kitchen and got his gut pounded by Jack Pratt's yo-yo.

The brothers began their morning run before the sun rose. They wheezed and huffed as they attempted to finish their push-ups. They almost vomited from the mayonnaise sandwiches Mr. Pratt promised would put five pounds of muscle on them. Their wrists felt as though they might break off from all the yo-yoing.

Jack Pratt smiled at their pain. The Yo-Yo Kid would be back soon and he would have a sidekick too. And Jack could die happy knowing he left behind a decent legacy. He could tell already the James boys had what it took. Or maybe he had just gotten less finicky in his old age. When he tried teaching a couple yo-yo champs a couple decades ago, they didn't seem to have the toughness and the fun loving attitude these two boys shared. But Jack remembered his wife was still alive and the kids would still visit then. Maybe he was now so desperate for company that he was kidding himself that these two boys had what it took. But then Jack Pratt doubted himself even further as he wondered if he really did reject a couple trainees or if he was just mistaking his life for an old Gregory Peck film again. Then he remembered his memory wasn't important. "Boys, come here." he yelled. They stopped their practicing and jogged over to their teacher. He tried tripping their feet with his yo-yo, but they were on to him, and they jumped over his trap.

"What do you want, Mr. Pratt?" Benny asked.

"Nothing boys." Jack Pratt said overcome with pride. "You're doing fine."

"Um... Mr. Pratt... you realize Benny and I still have to leave tomorrow, right?"

"What?" The old man said with great disappointment.

"Yeah... um... Jimmy's got school on Monday and I've got to go to L.A. to get ready for my TV special."

"School? TV? Is there any reason I lived this long? School's not going to get you anywhere and you just want to be on TV for the ladies. Let me tell you boys, I've lived a long life and nothing feels as good as saving a man's life. There's no other reason to live."

"Mr. Pratt, we appreciate everything you've done for us. Sharing your wisdom and your mayonnaise was really nice of you, but you didn't tell me anything over the phone. Did you expect us to train with you forever?"

Jimmy threw his two cents into the conversation. "Besides what can two guys with yo-yos do against gangs with guns?"

"I'll have you know in World War Two, we knocked... aahh, what's the point? I thought you two were different, but you boys are the same. Get out of my house."

"Mr. Pratt," Benny pleaded, "We don't have to hate each other. You've taught us a lot and I know with my yo-yo I can now defend myself from anyone, but..."

Mr. Pratt turned his back on his guests. Jimmy told his brother, "Forget about him. He's crazy."

"That's right. I'm crazy like a fox."

"What's that?" Jimmy asked in confusion.

"I'm crazy like a fox." And he whacked them both in the forehead with his yo-yos. "Now get back to work before I die." The two brothers weren't sure if their mentor forgot the discussion they had two seconds earlier, or if he was letting bygones be bygones. Either way they ran back to their training. "The yo-yo is like life." Mr. Pratt would shout. "It goes up and it goes down, but you're always in control."

The sixteenth time Benny heard this cluster of wisdom he realized what it meant. No matter what happens to you in life, you could always pretend it never happened and make up a better life. Benny made sure he and his brother humored Mr. Pratt, not out of respect, but out of pity. After all they might be the last animated objects that would listen to him in his lifetime. Benny figured after they left only the television would listen to Mr. Pratt's pearls of advice and criticisms.

When the day came, Saturday to be exact, that the boys had to head home, Benny went into the kitchen to try to break the news tenderly. But the old man wasn't in the kitchen, so he knocked on the bedroom door. Three knocks, no answer. Four knocks, still no answer. So Benny took the liberty of opening the door. He peeked in to see a body lying in the bed. "Mr. Pratt." Benny yelled. No answer. The most terrifying lump in his throat told Benny his host was dead. He ran to the body under the sheets and started shaking it. "Mr. Pratt? Jack! Simon!" He was spouting out names and names. Anything so he wouldn't be dead right now. And then, bang, the yo-yo got him right between the eyes.

And the old man was laughing in his bed. "I told you to always be ready for anything."

Benny touched the bridge of his nose where all the pain was screaming. His face was wet and when Benny glanced at the red on his fingers he shrieked, "I'm bleeding."

"Ahhh, it's nothing. Just a little mark for you to remember me. Don't want you being too pretty when you go to Hollywood. There's a lot of sissy boys there."

Benny was not upset because the scar might hurt his chances in Hollywood, he was more concerned that Kim might not be able to love someone with an open sore on his face. "You're crazy. And you're not crazy like a fox. You're crazy like an old man."

"No, I'm crazy like a fox. Because foxes are smart and old men aren't. So listen to what I have to say before you leave. And pretend I'm about to die because then what I'm saying will be more important to you." The old man stopped with a look of disgust and squirmed to get a tissue out of his pocket. "Here, wipe that blood off your face. It's disgusting." Benny did as he was told, but all the blood he saw on the tissue made it hard for him to listen. "First off Benny, your brother's an idiot. Don't ever listen to a thing he says. He's your sidekick. He listens to you. The second thing is movies and books have got it all wrong. You can have a million adventures and still not grow any wiser. It's all baloney that after something happens to you, you understand your life a little better. Even if you do come to an understanding about life, it won't make things any easier. So don't think you know anything or that you ever will know anything. Thirdly, don't trust any of the Friendlys. A Friendly destroyed the first Yo-Yo Kid, a Friendly will do the same to you. Fourth, don't tell anyone that I'm Jack Pratt or that I'm Simon Wiesel. And fifth, after you do tell someone my story, I want you to play me in the movie. Now, you and your brother get the heck out of here."

When Benny saw the old man wasn't joking Benny said, "Alright, Mr. Pratt. Thanks for everything."

"Don't forget what I told you."

"Don't worry Mr. Pratt I don't think I'll ever be able to forget about you." And Benny walked out the door.

He forgot about his bleeding until Jimmy freaked out about it, "Sheesh, what wall did you walk into?"

"Mr. Pratt and he said he wanted to see you too."

Jimmy walked into the house ready to kick the old man's butt if he tried anything violent on him. Two minutes later Benny's gullible little brother walked out of the house with a matching splotch of blood between his eyes.

"How did he get you?"

"I thought he was dead, so I shook him and he hit my head with his yo-yo and said to let dead ducks lie."

They walked back in the house to soap up their bruises to prevent infections just like their mother taught them. Then they left Arizona at speeds of up to 105.

Saturday, March 4, 1989
4:20 p.m.
Chapter Eleven

"No way man. That's going to take us so much longer."

"Mom's right. You do complain too much," Benny told his little brother. Jimmy's outburst occurred after Benny informed him that they were going back to the university, so that he could see Kim.

"Can you call this time to make sure she'll be there?"

"I don't need to. I can sense it."

"Oh now you've got a sixth sense? Is that what the crazy old man taught you? How to sniff someone from across the country? I would have pulverized that nut if he wasn't so close to dying anyway." Jimmy inspected the half moon shaped scar in the rear-view mirror. "Man, we should probably get stitches."

Benny didn't comment. Now that the blood had dried, he didn't mind his cut. It looked almost like a question mark between the eyes. Benny looked out at the desert road at the puddles that disappeared as you drove closer to them.

"Do you want me to drive?" Jimmy asked.

Benny shook his head. Jimmy might take them on a more direct route home. So Benny drove and reminisced about the time that would make this detour worth every extra second.

It was a beautiful day. As close to bliss as you were likely to get in this world. He and Kim were eating a picnic lunch under the shade of an oak tree. She laid her blond hair on his shoulder and told him, "It stinks. The only way I'll ever get to relive this day is by inventing a time machine. And then I'm going to have to kidnap my past self, tie her up in a room with food and water, just so I can spend this beautiful day with you again." And then they kissed. But then Benny remembered that didn't sound like something Kim would say. That was Jennifer who said that. He hated himself for committing such a blasphemous error. Benny blamed Jack Pratt for his contagious faulty memory. And he kept driving and driving stopping only for gas to keep the car going and black coffee to keep him going.

Benny felt great sympathy for Jack Pratt suddenly. It must be awful to not know what's real anymore. To not know if you're Jack Pratt or Simon Wiesel or none of the above. All the records and documents say one thing, but your memories and discreet birthmarks tell you you're someone else. Benny made a mental note to send Mr. Pratt a thank you note or a thinking of you card.

After many more mental notes which would be ignored later, they arrived at the cobblestone roads of beautiful State University. Benny remembered the old times as he drove past the familiar oaks and the lawns where he threw around the frisbee. Then he found a parking spot by her brick dormitory. He told his brother, "You can wait in the car if you want."

"I'm sick of the car. I'll see if I can chat up some pretty young thing and be a stud like my big brother."

With that Benny ran up the stairs and across the mildew carpets of the dorm's lobby. He found her door, room 103. There were two big nametags on the door, both in the shape of shamrocks. One said, Kim, the other, Rhonda. He prayed, prayed, prayed Kim was home as he knocked. God came through because after some unlocking, she was standing there just as he envisioned her all those hundreds of millions of times. But she looked different. Her short, blonde hair wasn't standing all over the place and she was a little skinnier, but still she was Kim, the girl of his dreams. So he swallowed her with a giant hug before she had time to think.

"Ben, Ben. What are you doing here?" she asked as he pushed them into her room. Her words didn't have much thought behind them. He always knew that, but she still smelled really good. Like strawberries. As he let go of her, he noticed they weren't alone. It was some lanky guy with thick glasses and exceptionally smooth skin. He was sitting on her bed and his hair was as messed up as Kim's. "Ben, what are you doing here?" She asked again with a smile which turned to a near scream as she wondered aloud, "Damn, what happened to your head?"

He looked at her and not her sensitive, poetry reading new lover, and gave her an answer. "My head? I bumped it. It's OK. I just smacked it while I was in Arizona. I just spent some time there and since it was on the way home I thought I would stop by and say hi."

'But isn't this like totally out of the way of Hatchet City?"

"No, I uh... found a shortcut." And the three of them stood there very silently. An introduction had to be made, so one was.

"Oh, Ben, this is Phil. Phil, you knew Betty right? Ben is her twin brother."

Ben wanted to throw up. This is how the love of his life introduced him? As somebody's twin brother? Ben shook his rival's hand. It was so smooth. No calluses. Ben figured Phil had never done a day's work in his life. Probably never spun a yo-yo either. Ben wanted to break Phil's slacker, hand in half, even though until he started yo-yoing, Benny never really worked either. Phil broke the ice of animosity. "So Ben, why were you in Arizona?"

"I don't know if Kim ever told you, but I was always very good with the yo-yo..."

"No. I never heard her mention your name before," Phil spoke in a phony British accent which made every word even more painful to Benny's ears.

"Well, I've become a pro yo-yoer. I won the world championships. Maybe you caught them on cable? If you didn't you can watch the TV special I'm filming in a few weeks. Anyway I was down in Arizona to really hone my yo-yo skills."

Kim laughed first. Phil followed once he realized what a smashing sense of humor Benny had. She slapped Benny's arm. "Aw, Ben, you're such a joker. What have you really been up to?"

Ben stopped hating Phil. He realized he never really knew Kim at all. She couldn't tell when Benny was telling a joke or when he was heartbroken and trying to reconcile true love. All this ache and pain, could it all have been for nothing? Worse than nothing since it probably killed his chances with Jennifer. Who by the way, Ben now realized was much prettier then what he thought was the ideal woman.

Go ahead Kim, take your high cheek-boned loser who felt no shame wearing the same clothes three days in a row. Benny's got something better lined up for him at home. He endured a bit more small talk with the couple while waiting for a convenient time to exit and get back on the road to his baby. But of course, as soon as it became obvious Ben was trying to back himself out of the conversation Phil abruptly said, "Oh no, it's five o'clock already. I've got to run. Nice seeing you Ben." He shook Ben's hand and said bye-bye to Kim, but curiously he didn't kiss her.

"Nice guy." Ben lied.

"Yeah, Phil is a good guy. He's Rhonda's new boyfriend. I introduced them at the open mike night at the coffeehouse. He's a killer poet." Well Ben figured at least he had the poet part right. Kim asked him, "Do you want to hear this poem I wrote?"

Benny said, "Yeah." Hoping it would be full of significance. Maybe it would push his life in some new direction like her love poems once did. She grabbed her journal, coughed twice, and read,

"What's the new craze?
Talking to yourself.
Everybody is doing it.
Why not join in?
You can be everything
And everybody or
Nothing and nobody.
What are you waiting for,
Someone else to start a
Conversation with you?"

"It's good" he told her. Then wondered, "Why did you choose that poem to read to me?"

"I wrote it this morning. You're the first person to hear it."

"Oh, I thought it was a comment on me or something."

She smiled.

"That's great. My professor says, good poetry should be universal. Everyone should feel it was written especially for them."

He wanted to ask her if she was as obsessed over him as he was over her. But he knew what the answer would be. He was just another passenger on her road trip through life. It didn't hurt Benny though because he knew his obsession was misplaced. It should have been reciprocated on someone who loved him too. So he asked Kim, "Your life is going alright? There isn't anybody you need me to rough up?"

She cracked up because she figured he was joking. He meant what he said though. He had grown proud of the warrior skills Jack Pratt taught him. "Ben, how did you get so funny? No, life's great. I'm so glad you knocked on my door. It's so good to see you can accept us being just friends. By the end I was scared you were turning into a stalker."

"Me too." He mumbled and it was so easy for him to hug her good-bye since his obsession had found a new target. Kim asked him to keep in touch and he would, but only in his memories.

Sunday, March 5, 1989
5:00 p.m.
Chapter Twelve

In case you had trouble figuring it out, this is a story about love. Really, all stories are about love. Romeo and Juliet. War and Peace. Peanut butter and jelly. Benny and some interchangeable blonde. First it was Kim, now it was Jennifer. The poor boy couldn't bear to be alone. So he was taking Stan Friendly's Mustang at speeds the law wouldn't permit anyone to go. When Benny's little brother asked him what the rush was, Benny responded, "I'm sick of the open road." But really he just wanted to see his baby. It was always Jennifer he was in love with, even before he knew who she was. Why else would he go out with a girl who looked so much like her? It was all starting to come together, but only inside Benny's mind. Nowhere else did it make as much sense.

See, he was born a shy, unassuming boy. He wasn't supposed to amount to much and he didn't. Every time he was tested, he failed. Until one day in high school he saw a couple kids, picking on a girl to the point of tears. Benny could have walked away like he did so many other times when he saw bullying, but he chose to do something about it. The only time he ever stood up for anyone. For his Jenny.

Then his life continued in a boring fashion. He majored in Communications at the university which he only attended because his twin sister was going there. Then he fell head over heels for the most beautiful girl he ever saw. But the reason he fell in love with Kim was because she looked so much like Jennifer. He thought Kim was what he was always looking for, but she was just a pale imitation. Saccharin to Jenny's sugar.

Then he met the real thing. Their love was so grand, it confused him. He thought he liked her because she reminded him so much of Kim, but that wasn't true. When he was with Kim, nothing happened. But

Jenny pushed him to the Amateur World Yo-Yo Championship. And she pushed him to find misguided wisdom.

And he pushed her away.

The shame pushed the gas pedal even harder. Benny was amazed how much sense life made in hindsight.

"Benny, do you think we're put on Earth for a reason?"

"What makes you ask that?" Benny asked his little brother with the fear that Jimmy had the power to read minds.

"We've talked about everything else the past week and I think we've beaten to death the argument over who's stronger, the Hulk or Superman. So I thought I'd ask what's on my mind."

Benny didn't need to put much thought into the question. "Yeah. Yeah. I think there's a reason we live."

"Well it's kind of messed up that the yo-yo is your reason to live."

"Is not."

"Is too. If anyone was ever born to do anything, you were born to play the yo-yo."

"No," Benny corrected him, "I'm here for something more important. The yo-yo is too silly a reason for me to exist."

If Jimmy wasn't at that age where everything he said had to be hip, if he could say one cheesy, sentimental thing during adolescence without hoping to have sex in return, it would be now when he would tell his brother, "You're right. You're not here to play with toys. You're here for moments like this." But Jimmy didn't say that. Wouldn't have been cool, so he watched the passing street signs until miles to Hatchet City reached zero.

Home. No more sleeping in the car. No more sleeping bags. A real mattress that you didn't have to share with a sweaty brother. But first Benny suggested, "How about we get a bite to eat?"

"Sounds cool. I hope Mom's got the fridge stocked."

Benny corrected himself, "No I meant we should go to Pretty Boy Floyd's and cap off the road trip with a little more brother time."

"Come on, Benny, who do you think you're fooling? You didn't get any from your old girlfriend so you want some from the new. Drop me off at home. I'm sick of this car."

If Benny could snap a neck and drive at the same time he would have a quadriplegic brother. But Benny kept his hands on the wheel and droppes his brother off at home. Then he steered himself to Pretty Boy Floyd's Bar and Grill. It was Sunday night. Not too many people hit the bar. Just the faithful. The ones who knew life could kick you down, but you could still enjoy a beer on the ground.

Benny entered with confidence and purpose. But his positive qualities wilted when he didn't see Jennifer tending bar. Instead there was that big bouncer behind the counter. Benny positioned his finger near his yo-yo in case he had to use it. Benny walked up to the bar. The bouncer made the first move. "Hey, hey, look who it is, Romeo himself."

"Where's Jennifer?"

"Ah, so you're looking for your Juliet. Well, I hope I can fit her shoes Romeo."

Benny tisked, 'Quit fooling."

"If you don't like me you're going to have to find another Juliet. Louie, how old is your daughter now? Maybe she'll do." The bouncer said to a drunk laughing out of his stool Benny wanted to see blood spouting out of the big guy's nicely manicured beard. "Your Juliet left town buddy. She went to Los Angeles… or was it New York? I can't remember. It was one of those places. They're not too big, so it shouldn't take too long for you to find her in one of them."

"What the heck do you have against me?"

"What I have against you Romeo, is you drove a good girl away from here. Ignoring her, playing her like a fiddle, you broke her heart."

Benny couldn't believe he was being chastised for insensitivity by a guy who pushed people out of bars for a living. There wasn't a chance the bouncer would be helpful so Benny walked away. He figured she probably left a message with his Mom and Dad anyway. The message would say where she went and they could make up with hugs and kisses and he would never touch a yo-yo again if that was what it took for them to be together.

Saturday, March 25, 1989
12:22 p.m.
Chapter Thirteen

Days distraught. Hole in the soul. Crying without any tears. Desperation and depression and it was all because of a girl. Just a speck in the universe and it was causing him more trouble than the asteroid that would de stroy the Earth in three million years. Benny figured by then intelligent beings would have created a giant robot to swat the asteroid away, but they still wouldn't have the cure for a broken heart. Everyone had tried to cheer him up. Jimmy begged Benny to go out and party with him. Dad brought out the ball and gloves to play some catch. Mom baked him a strawberry rhubarb pie. His old love, Kim even called him a few times to read poetry, but she was too little, too late. The only thing that distracted his heart from the pain for a couple minutes was a letter postmarked from Siberia.

Benny Boy,

Congrats on the Yo-yo championship. Mom told me you really kicked butt. Now you can afford to visit me. Siberia is still really cold, but we're doing a lot of good work. It gets frustrating sometimes. No matter how hard we work, the Siberians are still going to be cold. You wonder why they don't move and I wonder why I came here. But there must be some reason why the Peace Corps only approved my application to serve in Siberia. Well, only seventeen more months. Hang in there bro.

xoxo
Betty

But the attention from his sister didn't stop Benny from feeling awful. One night he wanted to purge all the sick, lonely feelings out of his stomach, so he stuck his head above the toilet. He looked down into the bowl and stuck his finger deep within his throat. As deep as it could go. The vomit trickled out slowly which only made him feel dirtier. After a thorough hand washing and tooth brushing, Benny layed in his bed and cried for days and nights and time went on.

Stan Friendly wanted to know where his soon to be household brand name star was hiding, so he called the James' household. Dad answered it, and forced Benny to accept the call. Benny fought and fought but ultimately he didn't have the strength to withdraw from the world. He grabbed the phone even though anyone's voice but Jenny's made him sick.

"Hello."

"Benny, my boy. Why do you sound so glum, chum?"

"Oh Stan, it's just personal things."

"Benny, I'm your manager. Nothing's too personal for me."

Ben thought about Stan's lineage and everything Jack Pratt taught him about the sinister ways of the Friendly clan, but then Benny remembered if Jack Pratt told the truth than Stan was really Jack Pratt's grandson. Secret relations aside, Benny suddenly felt the need to reveal to somebody, anybody, his secret heartbreak. "Aw Stan, my girl, Jenny, she.... She skipped town. She didn't say good-bye. She hasn't said anything. She hasn't even called. She just left me."

"That's rough kid. But let me tell you something, sitting around, dwelling on this girl doesn't do anything. She's not worth your tears, compadre. There's a lot of chicks in this coop we call the United States of America. You can't sit around and spend your nights thinking about her when there's so many women waiting for a prince of a guy like you. You need to keep busy and get your mind off her. Find a hobby... tell you what, why don't you come over for dinner? I've got a houseguest who's been dying to see you. So come over around eight."

"Sure." Ben surrendered. The will of Stan Friendly was too great. They hung up and Benny spent the next few hours singing along to the sad love songs playing on the radio.

Around seven-thirty, Benny got around to cleaning himself up. He felt obligated to look nice, but no matter how hard he scrubbed the soap against his skin, he still felt dirty. In a suit without a necktie Benny walked down the stairs.

Dad was sitting on his easy chair wondering, "Where are you headed Benny? Got a hot date?"

Benny was about to spill the beans but then he remembered what a broken heart felt like. His Dad might want acceptance from a sleazy boss instead of forgiveness from a sassy broad, but rejection still hurt no matter who dished it out. So Benny improvised with a nervous yell, "Dad, why aren't you ready?"

"Ready for what?" Dad looked over at Mom.

Mom shrugged her shoulders. She was paying more attention to the action thriller on TV. So Ben reminded him, "Remember? Dinner at Stan's house around eight? Ring any bells?" Benny couldn't believe he was following through with his lie.

"Tonight? I didn't know about this. Susan, did you?"

"Shhh. I'm trying to watch this." She said as she focused on the lone gunman on the roof.

"Dad, when you handed the phone to me, Stan asked if I was coming to dinner at his house with you tonight."

"He said that? Shoot. I always drone his voice out. Benny don't ever say yes without listening to the question."

"Yes sir."

Henry nagged his wife. "Come on Susan. Hurry up and get ready."

Benny saved his Mom from an evening of great awkwardness. "Um… Dad I don't think he mentioned Mom's name when he talked about coming over."

The commercial break started at the wrong time for Benny's web of lies. Now Susan James had entered the fray. "So Stan Friendly doesn't think I'm good enough for his parties?"

"No Mom. I just think it's a guy's night out kind of thing. You know cigars, beer, maybe some poker." Benny wasn't sure whether he liked his new habit of lying. But he figured he could smooth things over with his mother later.

So Dad drove his son to the Friendly estate. Dad copied his son's style of a jacket with no tie. Dad agreed a tie might be too dressy for this occasion which Benny only said because all his bowties were in the hamper.

Stan was surprised to see his accountant showing up with his prodigy. But Stan invited them both in after only skipping three beats. They entered the home slowly and Stan gave Henry the full tour that Benny had already received. Benny, meanwhile sat on the couch and wondered if he would have to be institutionalized. Doctors would have to poke at him and figure out why his heart always ached. It would be for the good of society.

"Am I interrupting something?" A feminine voice said which Benny assumed to be Mrs. Friendly. He turned around to see the voice belonged to his old rival at the yo-yo championships, Rebecca Monet. "You seem pretty lost in your thoughts."

She wasn't in her bikini. Instead she was in a relatively classy, maroon skirt and a loose, white blouse. Benny asked her, "What are you doing here?"

"That's the way you Midwesterners say hello? I thought this was a polite region of the country. I'm Stan's houseguest."

Looked like everyone provided a surprise visitor. Benny asked rudely, "What does his wife think of that?"

She was disgusted by his implication that without her sex appeal, there was no reason for her existence. "Stan's my agent. Not my pimp or sugar daddy. He flew me over here to discuss our future. Not that it's any of your business, but he's been a perfect gentleman." Privately Rebecca had her suspicions that Stan wanted some monkey business too, but he really had been a polite host.

And on that silent thought Stan entered the living room and said, "What are you guys standing around for? Let's eat."

Benny sat across from Cindy who earlier feigned anger when Benny kept addressing her as Mrs. Friendly. Next to Benny was Veronica, who would be oh so happy if anyone called her Miss Friendly. Oh man, the boys will be ragging on her last name when she gets to high school. But right now high school was the least of Veronica's concerns or anyone else's at the dinner table. Benny was thinking about love. His father was thinking about which fork should be used to eat the salad.

Stan was thinking about the company whose stock he just bought. His wife was thinking about vacationing in Switzerland in the summer. Their daughter thought about the platform shoes she just bought which had her standing at five feet even. Rebecca was thinking about not wearing her bikini when she performed any more, since it was giving her an awful reputation.

It wasn't a silent, contemplative dinner as all this thinking would suggest. There were jokes and laughter and tummy rubbing but there were enough silent moments for everyone's heads to wander someplace else. There would be only one other moment when all these people would be in the same room at the same time again. The next time, everyone's mind would be at the same place, but for tonight other people and matters seemed more important than the present company.

For example, the issue of Benny's sadness. His feelings were brought to everyone's attention over the chocolate mousse by Stan. "Veronica, honey, our friend Benny is sad. What should he do to not be sad?"

She shrugged her bony shoulders. "I don't know. Watch cartoons?"

"There you go Benny. Even a ten-year-old girl knows you need to do something. Isn't that right Hank?"

Benny's Dad hated being called Hank. His Mom named him Henry. Hank was a name for truck drivers and country music stars. Not a name for a respectable accountant, but it was his employer calling him that so he swallowed his pride and answered, "When you're right, you're right. Stan."

"So you see, Benny, it's unanimous. You've got to do something to get your mind off that girl. How about you start with getting drunk?" Stan poured some Chardonnay in Benny's glass. Benny drank it in no time flat and then another and another and the night did grow merrier. And the wine got sweeter. And Rebecca Monet started resembling more and more the most beautiful girl in the world even if her hair was much larger and filled with hairspray.

Benny stared at her with an open mouth and wondered if maybe Rebecca and Kim were really Jennifer in disguise. He had never seen

Jenny in the same room with either of these two blondes and stranger things had been known to happen, like him being a yo-yo champion. But as Benny finished that thought he and his father were politely kicked out of the Friendly house. Benny didn't even fully realize that they had eaten another round of dessert and watched some powerboat racing on TV. He just noticed his wine glass was constantly empty and was constantly being replenished. There were good-byes and then Dad took the steering wheel because he was slightly less drunk than his son.

"Benny, have I told you how proud I am of you?" The father told the son.

Benny made no reply because he was shocked by the resemblance his father shared with a turtle. If his Dad was just a little greener and had a shell, he could be a pet.

"Your mother and I, we were always worried about you. We always thought Betty was the family winner and we'd have to take care of you for the rest of your life. Either that, or you would end up in some thankless bureaucratic position like your old man. You just never showed any passion. Turns out it may be your brother, your Mom and I will have to take care of forever. Guess, accountants aren't good at counting their chickens before they hatch."

Benny smiled at his father, the slow reptile who managed to beat the hare.

"And Ben…Stan's right. You've got to forget Jennifer. Before I met your Mom I was in the gutter. This girl, Vanessa, she left me for some rich jerk. All I wanted was to play my clarinet in a jazz band and she saw I had no future so she went for the thirty-year-old accountant with the pension and vacation time and… Well, I threw away my clarinet and went back to school and eventually became a thirty-year-old accountant with the girl. And… and it all turned out OK. I met your Mom and we had you and Betty and Jimmy, but I guess… I guess it turned out alright."

Benny nodded and the car felt warm with contentment. But the warmth escaped with the passengers' bodies as they reached their home. As the night grew later Henry surprised his wife with affection that she hadn't experienced in much too long. Meanwhile Benny sat in his room and ached. His lonely life was wasting away and there was nothing he could do about it. There were moments where the pain was distracted, but for the most part it was as much a part of his life as the question mark scar between his eyes.

Then his mind flashed back to the Arizona sun where Mr. Pratt told him time and time again, "Nothing feels as good as saving a man's life." So Benny opened his window.

Right before he swung out he remembered he needed a mask. It couldn't be too obvious that he was The Yo-Yo Kid. Nothing convenient in his room, but then he remembered the basement, where his Mom kept the Spider-man mask she had proudly sewn for Benny on a Halloween past. Benny ran down the stairs, fit the snug mask over his head and decided there was no point in climbing up to the second floor just so he could swing down. Instead Benny just ran out the front door all the way to the only place where there might be trouble, Pretty Boy Floyd's Bar and Grill.

Sweat pouring down his masked face and adrenaline pumping through his bloody veins, Benny had the scent of an absolute maniac to anyone within smelling distance. Benny clung to the midnight shadows so no passing cars could see him sprinting to town to avenge evil deeds. But when he reached the bar absolutely nothing was going down. Benny realized he'd have to be lucky to spot a crime. Even though a thousand crimes take place a day, Benny couldn't remember too many that he ever witnessed. There was the time in elementary school when he saw kids stealing candy from the five and dime. In college one night, a friend backed into a parked car and left without leaving a note. But Benny only once witnessed a felony. It was when he let Jenny slip through his fingers.

Benny squatted behind a blue van with a painting of a Valkyrie on its side. As Benny watched one drunk after another walk to their cars he reminisced about that late night they spent together. The one where Jenny reached over him to grab her purse and pulled out two cigarettes. One was for him. One for her. He refused as she lit up. The smoke clung to her sweaty body and she kept pestering him to defy the surgeon general's warnings. "Come on. It's always been my dream to smoke a cigarette and talk about life and philosophy with my sweetheart." Benny couldn't fight peer pressure like that. At that moment he would have hacked out a thousand coughs to thank Jenny for giving him the illusion that he was back again with Kim. Stupid. Stupid. Stupid.

"What do you want out of life?" she asked. Her breath was awful due to the tobacco.

"Love," Benny said.

"Love. You're so easy to please, baby. Cause you've got my love. I wish I was as easy as you."

"What makes you so complicated? What is it you want?" Benny asked her in resentment.

"I don't know and it's making me restless. I know there's something to life that we all need, but I can't figure it out. There are seconds where I feel it and then it goes away without telling me what it is. But look at me baby, you're making me ramble." She then showered him with kisses. A cleaner shower he never had. At the time he was thinking she was calling him baby sarcastically. Maybe she meant it?

She was getting somewhere that day when they were figuring out life. She was teaching him how, "Our souls have all these magical properties. That's why I love acting so much. I get to put myself in someone else's soul. It's such a rush and sometimes when I'm working I get that giddy feeling too. When alcohol isn't making people awful, it can really get people to open themselves up." She was so wise. Why did she leave? Shoot… Benny just noticed while he was lost in thought most of the cars had disappeared.

There was only one car in the lot, the van with the spray-painted Valkyrie on her horse. If Benny really squinted he could make her look like Jenny. Who else could own this van, but that big jerk of a bouncer? Benny was ready to kill. He was ready to save. He was ready to do the right thing. As the big guy walked to his van, Benny snuck around the side with far from perfect footwork. The bouncer turned his head at the sound of shuffling feet in time for a red yo-yo to clock his temple. It brushed the bouncer back and greatly irked him.

"What the…?"

Another yo-yo clocked him and then another and then the bouncer grabbed one of the yo-yos in mid-air and pulled Benny by the string, closer to him. "I'm going to kill you… Spider-man?" Benny was glad he brought a third yo-yo and that all his yo-yo's had breakaway strings. He clocked the bouncer with a right hand yo-yo and wrapped the string around his neck with the left.

"Where is she? What did you do to her?" Benny asked.

The bouncer hacked and coughed as it was difficult to talk with a string choking your life away and a metal yo-yo constantly battering your head. Benny loosened the chokehold.

"I'll ask you again. Where is she?"

"I don't know, Spider-man. Who do you mean?"

"Jenny. Jennifer."

"Oh Lordy, it's you, Romeo?" Benny banged the bouncer again. "Stop that." The bouncer yelled. "If you promise not to hit me again, I'll tell you."

Benny smacked him one more time and then relented, "OK. I promise." His yo-yos came back to him.

"And take off that mask too, you maniac. You're not Spider-man."

"You're right. I'm The Yo-Yo Kid."

"Cripes." The bouncer said for the umpteenth time. "Can't you understand you ruined it with her? Learn from it and treat the next girl you fall in love with some dignity."

"No. There's no next girl. There's only Jenny."

The bouncer leaned against the van and rubbed all the bumps on his head. "Listen, take off the mask and I'll talk." Benny reluctantly obliged. "She didn't leave any forwarding address, but she said she was leaving to LA." Benny's heart sparkled with joy since that's where he would be in less than a month. "So you think you can teach me how to beat someone up with a yo-yo?" The bouncer asked, but it was too late. The Yo-Yo Kid had fled for the day had been saved.

Tuesday, April 25, 1989
11:00 a.m.
Chapter Fourteen

"It's showtime kid. Go out there and knock 'em dead." Stan said as he barged into Benny's private dressing room

Kill them.

Benny was in the mood to do just that. Go down into the studio audience and kill as many of those purposeless people as his yo-yos could handle before the cops started shooting. But Benny knew he couldn't do that because he would feel too guilty for the victims' grandchildren and all the puppies that would be orphaned.

Benny looked into the mirror and wished himself luck. The stylist added a touch of mousse to his hair which was growing a bit longish. Stan suggested he grow his hair out to look a little hipper. He also really pushed Benny to get an earring to make him look a little more dangerous, but Benny couldn't stand the thought of a needle piercing a hole through his skin. So Stan was dreaming up hundreds of other ways to give yo-yos some status in this era of extremes.

Benny rehearsed in his mind all the action they had been choreographing for the past week. The cameras were all in their proper positions so Benny couldn't miss his cues by even a quarter of an inch or the cameras might not capture his poetry in motion.

In the past month in spite of all the time spent preparing for his television debut and the occasional nights of vigilantism, Benny had a birthday. He turned 23. That was his last hope. He was sure if Jenny would ever call him, it would be on his birthday. But the phone stayed silent as he waited patiently by its side. It was sad and somewhat pathetic, but every time he left to use the bathroom or to heat up some split pea soup, he would constantly run back to the phone because he was sure he heard ringing. But no, she didn't call and let him know that someone was thinking about him.

His yo-yo loved him though. She had a name now too, like any loved one should. Her name was Jenny. It was symbolic because even though she left him for what at times seemed like an eternity she always found her way back.

The show's director yelled, "Action" and Benny went through the magic motions. No matter how many times you saw Benny James play the yo-yo it always felt like the first time. It was like preparing to jump into a cold river. You could imagine the coldest cold, but it wouldn't compare with the sensation of plunging in.

You could replay Benny's mastery a hundred thousand times in your head, but when you actually saw the impossible, all preconceptions of reality disintegrated.

One yo-yo stood in the air forever. Another did a loop. Another went around the world. Another bounced in and out of his hand. Four yo-yos spinning at once by a man with only two hands? Impossible? Yes, but it was on TV so it had to be real. Unlike the rest of Benny's life that didn't have objective cameras to record every moment, this day of his life would be edited into a prime-time half hour for the world to enjoy.

Benny strutted and asked for his beautiful assistant to join him onstage. It was Rebecca Monet in a sequined dress. At first she was a bit peeved that she was billed as Benny's assistant instead of getting her own time slot which was what Stan promised her. But then all her wise advisors told her this could lead to many more opportunities than waiting tables or entering more yo-yo competitions. All her petty jealousies receded when she walked on stage and was greeted with warm, buttery applause.

She showed off her yo-yo skills and then in a Stan Friendly approved Southern accent she drawled, "Not bad for a girl, huh?" Laughter from the drones.

Then they did some swordfighting, using yo-yos instead of swords. Rebecca seemed to have the upper-hand, but Benny had to win. He was the star. So when Benny was backed into a corner with no place to go, he spun his yo-yo around a flagpole conveniently placed overhead and swung over her. Then he wrapped her up with the yo-yo in his left hand. She cursed, "Drats, foiled again." And Benny continued tempting fate by attempting yo-yo stunts no mere mortal should accomplish. He was Babe Ruth. He was Michaelangelo. He was Jesus of Nazareth. He was The Yo-Yo Kid.

Saturday, August 26, 1989
3:52 p.m.
Chapter Fifteen

"Yeah, Mom." Benny said over the telephone. She had a thousand questions and Benny did his best to oblige her with one-word answers. He was resting on the balcony of a San Francisco hotel room. His view overlooked Union Square, but he wasn't looking down. His eyes were fixed up at the fastest moving clouds he ever did see.

"And Stan's making sure you get enough food? I can tell from your father's paychecks what a penny pincher he is."

"Yes, Mom."

"And you're happy?"

"Yes, Mom." No son could tell his mother he was not happy. It's a slap in her face after carrying you for nine months. "Is Jimmy there? You think I can talk to him?"

"Only if you promise to talk some sense to him. The principal called that he was skipping class on his first week of school. Jimmy, get over here, your superstar brother wants to talk to you."

"Mom!" Benny whined out of embarrassment.

"What? You are a superstar, my dear, and you always have been to me."

She was kind of right. After the incredible ratings of Benny's television performance. Stan put together a makeshift tour of North America where Benny and Rebecca basically reenacted their television performance in small theaters.

"Here he is." Mom told Benny. "Take care."

"Yo, what's up Benny."

"Mom tells me you've been getting in trouble."

Suddenly sunshine radiated through Benny's telephone all the way from Hatchet City as Jimmy spoke, "Dude you would have been so proud of me. I played such a Don Juan. This new girl from California, she's so California, she's always saying, 'right on'. She sat next to me in

English class and after class she asks, 'Do you know where room 232 is?' So I said, "Sure do. My next class is there.' And she said, 'Right on. Me too.' And so the rest of the day I kept pretending I was in her class. And then she drove me home in her car. It kind of stinks that they called Mom just because I went to the wrong classes, but it was so worth it."

Benny was glad to hear such giddiness. It reminded him of his time with Jenny which in turn reminded him to ask, "Do you ever see Jenny's sister at school?"

"Michelle? Yeah she hangs with the football players and the cheerleaders."

"Can you do me a favor?" Jimmy gagged because he knew what was coming. "Can you ask Michelle for her sister's phone number?"

"You don't give up Benny, do you?"

"Not on Jenny and not on my yo-yo."

Jimmy laughed. Once in a while his big brother could be pretty alright. "You still going out at night with your mask and yo-yo?"

"As long as there's crime, it's Yo-Yo Kid time." Benny was now officially in a silly mood. A very different mood from the night before when he was walking along Mission Street and heard that scream from the second floor. Benny swung up the fire escape and smashed open a window after witnessing a brute smacking his wife. All the innocent deserved the Yo-Yo Kid's protection, so Benny beat up the oppressor real good. Then he asked what he always asked, "Where is Jenny Royce? Tell me or I'll make you cry."

That time the criminal didn't speak English so Benny asked, "Donde esta Jenny Royce?" No answer came so Benny bashed in the criminal's head with the yo-yo and then ran away looking for more evil doers.

But the bad guys never had the answer. Sometimes they had guns, but Benny learned how to deflect bullets with his yo-yo. If his yo-yo blocked the bullet with enough topspin, the bullet would swerve. But Benny couldn't see a point in accomplishing superhuman feats if he didn't have anyone to share them with. The way he shared those smiles with Jenny that would grow wider and wider as they stared at each other's goofy grins. Sometimes when she was really hyper she would jump into his body and hug him not just with her arms but also with her legs. It was a trusting move because Benny could have dropped her. But he never did. Not once.

Jimmy broke into Benny's nostalgia, "Benny did I tell you what happened the other day? I was mowing the front lawn and I noticed across the street a white Cadillac. I moved as close to the car as I could without being too obvious and I saw an old guy sitting in the car."

"Mr. Pratt?"

"No that's what I thought at first. But this guy was even older. And I think he was spying on me because as I got closer the car started and he made a real quick u-turn so he wouldn't have to drive by me."

An interesting turn of events. Benny had been thinking about Mr. Pratt quite a bit. He tried calling a few times but never got an answer. Benny wondered if Stan might steer the tour toward Arizona. Benny could use a good story.

Over the phone Benny could hear some commotion. Jimmy explained, "Mom wants me to do some homework. Mom, idleness is not the devil's tool. If it wasn't for lazy days Benny never would have mastered the yo-yo. Ain't that right Ben?"

"Listen to Mom, Jimmy."

"Alright. Make me proud on Friday. I'm throwing a party for all the cool kids to watch you on the Late Night Show."

They hung up and Benny took a nap. His performance wasn't until much later and not too many crimes took place between three and five in the afternoon. So he rested. With sleep came a mid-afternoon dream that blurred reality away.

Benny was awakened by Stan's firm hands. "Come on my boy, it's showtime. Go out there and earn that money out of the rubes' hands."

Benny threw on his bowtie and tuxedo coat. He ran in the direction Stan pointed. But instead of popping into an avant-garde theater, Benny was standing on the woodchips of an outdoor circus freak show. There was the two headed man, the fat woman who caught cannonballs in her bellybutton, the geek who bit off chicken heads, midgets, and hundreds of other genetic anomalies. But they weren't Benny's co-stars. They were the audience. And the barker with his top hat was Jack Pratt. And he was shouting in an exaggerated Romanian accent, "Come one, come all and see the biggest freak in our solar system. A man who can do nothing but play with the yo-yo. Can he interact with other people? No. Can he satisfy a lover? No. Can he come up with his own identity? No. He must steal the name, The Yo-Yo Kid. Yes, ladies and gentlemen, stare while you can. A freak like this is a once in a lifetime spectacle."

Friday, December 1, 1989
2:21 a.m.
Chapter Sixteen

As the profits and the media exposure kept growing, so did the length of the Yo-Yo Express Tour. Stan wanted to milk his 33 trick ponies for all they were worth, Benny and Rebecca didn't have anything or anyone on the backburner at home so they didn't put up much of a fuss as they swung through Middle America and started up the East Coast. The day before was Tampa. Tonight was Miami Beach. The cities were all blurring together, but Benny made it a point to punish at least one criminal in every town.

Earlier that evening he packed the Jackie Gleason Center for Performing Arts. Benny worried that the venues were getting too big. How could the people in the back possibly see what he was doing with his yo-yo?

Stan told him, "They didn't pay to see your yo-yo, stupid. They paid to see you."

Benny hated being called stupid. He also hated being recognized when he was out fighting crime. Some pretty young woman sucking a lollipop while holding her boyfriend's arm said, "I know you."

"No you don't." Benny kept looking for trouble. Washington Avenue at 2 am was still loaded with club kids and other ne'er-do-wells that he could hurt.

"Sure, you're the yo-yo guy. I saw you on that soap opera."

"You must be mistaken." Benny kept walking. No one should be able to recognize him in his Zorro mask and he never should have agreed to play himself on that stupid, stupid TV show.

"Come on. Do one trick for us."

"Do you know Jennifer Royce?" He figured it was worth a shot. "Who?"

And that was all Benny needed to completely ignore one of his fans. He picked up the pace. There was so much scum around.

Somebody had to be up to something sinister. He took a left into an alley but got tripped up. His face hit the concrete and before the pain of a split lip registered in his cerebral cortex a loud thwack echoed against his spine. Then he felt the unmistakeable pain of an oak yo-yo smacking the back of his head. And then he lost consciousness.

It came back for a couple seconds, Benny couldn't see and started mumbling incoherently which earned him another smack from a yo-yo.

Then cold water fell upon him. It was like electricity injected into his bloodstream. A bright, blinding light greeted Benny. He wanted to escape the light, but his legs and arms were tied with yo-yo string to the chair he was sitting on. Benny yelled, "Help! Help!"

Then a yo-yo came out of the light and crushed his forehead.

"You shut up if you know what's good for you."

Benny thought he knew that voice. "Mr. Pratt? Mr. Pratt? Is that you, you crazy freak. Let me out of here."

The yo-yo hit him again. "You do not know me."

"Mr. Pratt, why are you doing this?"

"Stop calling me Mr. Pratt. I am Simon Wiesel."

And the light was turned off. Benny could almost see again. Slowly his pupils returned to normalcy and he saw a frail, old man in a wheelchair. He had no hair, not even eyebrows, and his face was much sterner than Mr. Pratt's. Next to the old man were two faces Benny did know. Edgar Jones, Benny's runner-up at the Yo-Yo Championship and Javier Hernandez, a semifinalist. Looked like they had been working out since that remarkable day almost a year earlier.

The old, old man was talking and Benny realized it was his battered ears that made him sound like Jack Pratt. "What you have been doing goes completely against our rules."

"What rules?" The dried blood on Benny's lip was making it difficult for Benny to speak.

"You don't know any of the rules? That idiot Pratt."

"Who are you?" Benny asked.

"That's enough out of you." Edgar said and smacked Benny in the head again.

"Stop it you moron." The old man screamed at Edgar. He took a breath and gave Edgar a couple dollars. "Go get some coffee, donuts."

Edgar nodded his head leaving Benny wishing his tongue was longer so he could lick his wounds. The old man began talking again. His accent was thick making it difficult for Benny's cauliflower ears to pick up the information. "What has Jack Pratt told you?"

"What do you mean?"

Without warning a yo-yo spun out of the geezer's hand, floated the length of the room, and collided with Benny's nose. Benny never saw a yo-yo move like it had its own mind before. His first words after ouch were, "You are Simon Wiesel."

"Yes and what has that senile man told you?"

"He told me everything. He said he was really you and was just pretending to be Jack Pratt. Would you mind telling me what's going on and why you're beating me up?"

The old man wheeled in his direction. "I am Simon Wiesel. I am the Yo-Yo Kid."

"I believe you. I saw your films at Stan Friendly's house."

A yo-yo struck Benny's face. "Don't ever mention that name again. A pox on the Friendly Clan. His grandfather..."

"Actually, " Benny broke in, "Mr. Pratt is Stan's grandfather."

"No, you idiot. I am Stan's grandfather. Everything Jack Pratt told you about himself is really my story. He's a liar. I only put up with him because he's rich. But he will die and go to hell soon enough."

The novelty was wearing off and the pain was kicking in so Benny bluntly asked, "Can you please tell me why you kidnapped me?"

"I will let Jack Pratt answer that question for you. I will be watching you." And with that a spinning yo-yo brought Benny back to sleep. He woke up on a sidewalk in Miami Beach as the sun rose above the Atlantic Ocean. His face was bloody and broken and he limped along with the pigeons to his nest.

Benny slept for many hours and then knocked on the hotel room next door. Stan opened immediately. Before Stan was given a chance to ask why his meal ticket was all battered and bruised, Benny said, "Stan, I can't tour any more."

"You're a mind reader Benny. But you should let your mind focus more on keeping your face away from runaway trains. What happened, my boy? Do you owe some mobsters some money?"

Benny couldn't put into words what happened if he wanted to. He just knew he needed to focus on other things besides entertaining America's bored spectators. He needed to find Jenny and Jack Pratt and answers. He told Stan, "I'm fried. I'm done."

"You are done Ben. After tonight, tomorrow in Orlando and Saturday in Tallahassee then we'll take a month off for the holidays. I could tell you were getting tired."

"No, Stan. I'm done now."

"Ben, I can believe you would do this to me. Even after all the work I've done for you. I can understand you doing this to Rebecca even after she left her ego at the door so you could be the star. But I can't believe you would do this to yourself. You'll never be a household name of fame if you don't get around."

Ben didn't care about fame, but for some reason he backed down. "Alright. Three more shows and that's it." Things were getting out of control. Everything was a fight now even the things that weren't worth fighting for. Maybe Betty was the smart one. She left it all behind for Siberia where all your troubles freeze into ice cubes.

Tuesday, December 5, 1989
3:31 p.m.
Chapter Seventeen

"Come out Mr. Pratt, I know you're in there." Benny banged on that Arizona window. Benny didn't feel like returning home. Too many unanswered questions left hanging in the air. So after winding up the tour with a packed house in Tallahassee, Benny booked a flight to the great Southwest to the dry heat and to the hiss of scorpion stings. "Open the door Mr. Pratt or I'll break it down. I can hear you watching your stupid game shows."

A hushed voice came from the other side of the door.

"Who is it?"

"You know who I am. But all I know about you is you're crazy."

The door slowly unlocked and the old timer whispered, "Shhh… Keep your voice down. They're watching." Jack Pratt's hair was a mess. He had on sweatpants and a Chicago Bears sweatshirt. "Do you want a mayonnaise sandwich, Benny?"

"No! I don't want your stupid food. I want to know how you can be Simon Wiesel and be so nice to me and how there can be another Simon Wiesel who kidnaps me and beats the heck out of me."

"Oh." The old man said as he settled into his easy chair and offered his guest some prune juice. After Benny waved off the drink, Jack Pratt pleaded, "Please sit down." Benny did as he was told and Jack Pratt asked, "What exactly did this so-called Simon Wiesel say to you?"

Benny exploded. "You're the so-called Simon Wiesel. This nut who tied me up was the real deal. And he hinted that you might be next. So it might be in your best interest to clue me in on what's happening."

Benny thought a false sense of urgency might loosen the truth off of Jack's tongue, but the old liar's attention was focused on Daily Dilemma's special question of the day. "Mayonnaise. The answer is mayonnaise."

The television personality confirmed Mr. Pratt's guess. "Mayonnaise is the correct answer."

Benny lost faith. Would things ever make sense or would life always be so jumbled that only madmen have the answers he needed? Benny got up to leave and continue his search for Jenny. "Alright Mr. Pratt, it was a pleasure to see you again."

Benny started to walk away but again a yo-yo smacked the back of his scalp. "Sit down boy. We've got to have a talk."

On no other occasion would Benny have been so pleased to have a scab broken. Benny looked past Mr. Pratt's saggy eyelids into his reddened, glassy eyes and begged, "Tell me the truth. The real truth."

"Where should I start?"

"With the truth."

"Alright. I'm not Simon Wiesel. I mean sometimes I am. Someone has to be. But my parents didn't name me Simon. They named me Jack Pratt, born in Chicago, Illinois. My old man was a drunk. My Mom didn't want me to end up like him, so she was always on my case to get good grades and I did. Got me a poor boy's scholarship to the University of Chicago. I studied journalism. Ended up third in my class and got married to a girl I met at a mixer. There you happy? That's the truth."

"Then what happened, sir?"

"My wife died. She was pregnant and she died."

"Gosh, I'm sorry."

Silence until the old man changed his tune. "I'm sorry. I lied again. She wasn't pregnant, but she did die. Polio. She left me real rich though, I wouldn't have to work no more, but then what would I have done? So I continued working as a freelance reporter covering the issues of the day. It was an exciting time to be alive, but I didn't want to live anymore. I was like you Benjamin, a romantic. What was the point of living, if the one person I enjoyed sharing life with no longer existed? World War II came around that time. I wanted to serve but my asthma kept me from serving on the front line. Instead I wrote about the boys overseas. And I did cover the Yo-Yo Brigade including the real Simon Wiesel. He was a loner which drew me to him. I could tell he had a hell of a story, and he did. I told it to you. Took me years to pick all that information out of him. He was worse off than me."

"How so?"

"You should have seen Simon fight. He wasn't very big, in fact he was so skinny and wiry, he looked like he ran on electricity. He enjoyed getting hurt. He said it reminded him he was alive. A crazy man if I ever met one. I asked him one sleepless night if there was anything besides pain which gave him pleasure. He said saving a life. I asked him what if the man whose life you saved was as miserable as he was? He said that was even better. Then without warning he wrapped his bony hands around my neck. I tried to fight him off, but I was weak and he was electric. I was sure the last sight I would ever see would be his ugly, scarred mug. Everything got dizzy. My ears popped and then he let go. I coughed until I cried and he stood over me and said, 'How does it feel to know you would be dead, if I hadn't saved your life? I know I feel good.'

"He proved his point. When faced with death, life always gets better. Forgive the sentimentality, Benjamin, but after that occasion I viewed Simon less as a man and more as a force of nature. He had the passion of a thunderstorm. The meaninglessness of a wave. Even after he tried to kill me I couldn't stay away from him. We talked about how we could get more people to feel the satisfaction of saving a life. We came up with the idea of a civilian Yo-Yo Brigade. A secret society that prowled the streets, saving humanity from itself.

"I would be the second member because Simon liked me much more than the soldiers the army enlisted for the military Yo-Yo Brigade. They were machines, and I was a human being who could appreciate the greatest of good deeds. And thanks to my wife I was a rich human being that could fund a team of heroes.

"But then the Yo-Yo Brigade was sent on a top-secret mission. No press was allowed to come along. So I worked on my story when it was suddenly killed. The story and the Yo-Yo Brigade were bombed to hell. The magazine's policy was no stories that might demoralize the general population. I quit out of protest. Simon Wiesel and the Yo-Yo Brigade was a story that should have been told, but none of the cowards would print it. I came back to the States destitute and..."

"Wait Mr. Pratt, quit lying. You said you inherited tons of money from your wife."

"Destitute in spirit, you wisenheimer. When you have nothing, money is nothing. No wife. No family. No one to teach me how to save people's lives. I lived in a rundown hotel in Chicago and every day grew more and more sickening. I ate at a diner on the corner which was where I saw his face. He looked like any other down and outer who would occupy a booth and only buy a cup of coffee, but it was Simon Wiesel. 'Sit down' he said.

"'Simon Wiesel is that you?' I asked. He had a thick beard so I couldn't be sure, but I was sure when he told me to sit down again. 'I thought you were dead'

"'Simon Wiesel is dead.' He told me the story I told you, that he took the luckiest poop in humanity's history and while everyone else was bombed to bits he remained intact and decided to switch dogtags with some poor sap named Ronald Ranch. He didn't want the government to be able to track him down again. Especially if we were going to start an illegal Yo-Yo Brigade. When he uttered those words life came back to me. Every day he showed me the tricks, the moves, and the power any Yo-Yo Kid should have. And at night we put our moves to use. We kicked some serious tush. Everything was great then one night Simon said, 'You're ready.' I didn't know what he meant. 'You are ready for me to leave Jack. Chicago is safe in your hands.'

"He was breaking my heart and scaring me. I couldn't do it alone. The city was too big. He told me the world was too big. There were too many people out there who would die without the thrill of knowing another person was alive because of you. He gave me a great pep talk which kept me motivated for two years. Then I started taking an occasional night off, which became a couple nights off which became only working my night job on the weekends. Then I stopped. I got tired of exhilaration. After two years the thrills, the chases, the knowledge that for every villain punished there were five more waiting to take his place got to be too much.

"Then the diner I always ate at went up for sale. I bought it. The old owner couldn't see why I was eating at this greasy spoon if I could afford my own restaurant. I told him to mind his own business and to hand over the deed. He couldn't understand the beauty of secret identities. Apparently with the deed came the marrying rights to the best looking waitress. Rita wouldn't give me the time of day before I showed signs of prosperity. I called her a gold digger, but she showed me a good time. She was no Jane… my first wife, and I never failed to remind her of that, but it was time to settle down. Hardly anyone gets to settle up. We had two kids and they were the only ones who played with yo-yos.

"Then one night I was short staffed so I served as back-up waiter. And when I brought out a fried mackerel to table eight I saw a face I hadn't seen in ten years. Clean shaven and worn down it was Simon Wiesel. He asked why I let him down. I told him it got to be too much. I wanted normalcy. I was sick of people owing me their lives. He complimented my fish and told me to sit down. Even though customers from every corner screamed for service I complied. He told me I was right. We needed more Yo-Yo Kids and he knew how to find them.

"We started a Yo-Yo Championship to see which kids had the mettle to become heroes. That idea was a failure. Turned out kids who spend too much time with yo-yos generally tend to be antisocial misfits who aren't much good at following our orders. After all these disappointing recruits who couldn't save a widow from a teddy bear, Simon and I decided to close up shop. But a couple other of Simon's Yo-Yo Kids decided to keep the Championships going. I wouldn't give them a nickel so they turned to corporate sponsors and the Championships turned into the sorry state you see today. But Simon, myself, and some other factions still use the Championships as a farm system to find new Yo-Yo Kids."

Benny was so proud of him. "See, Mr. Pratt, you had an amazing life. There was no reason you had to lie to me before. I mean, you were telling the truth right now, weren't you?"

"As far as I know." His eyes returned to the television screen.

Benny wasn't through with questions. "When Mr. Wiesel had me tied up he said I was breaking the rules. Do you know any rules?"

"Ahhh… let's see if I can remember them. That old fascist loved rules. One was never run away from a cry for help. Another was only fight with yo-yos because any other weapon invites defeat. Oh, then you're only allowed to patrol your assigned city."

"Wait... I was never assigned a city."

"Sure. You got your whatchamacallit... Hatchet City."

"But nothing ever happens in Hatchet City."

"Well its got to be your home town. Where will you be living?"

Wherever Jenny is. "I haven't decided."

"Well, make your decision. I've got to register it with that fascist Wiesel. It's a whole, long process. Oh, by the way Simon probably doesn't take too fondly to your career as a yo-yo performer. He doesn't want any attention being drawn to his Yo-Yo Brigade."

"Jeez! Thanks for telling me all this before."

"You're welcome. Thanks for sticking around for the duration of your training."

"You're welcome." Benny said and then there were grunts and icy stares. But as soon as the television started broadcasting commercials, all was forgiven and forgotten.

"Benjamin, do you want some pickled herring?"

"No thank you sir."

"You are staying the night though, aren't you?"

"If you don't mind. I'm tired of travelling."

"Alright. I'll keep the herring on ice."

Wednesday, March 7, 1990
5:53 p.m.
Chapter Eighteen

The hammock swung Ben back and forth as he watched the clouds above move in unison. He wondered about how there were waves smacking into America and at the same time there were waves smacking into the coast of Portugal. There must be some epicenter in the middle of the sea where all those waves began and that was where Benny James wished he was.

Some extra weight dropped on to the side of the hammock. Benny moved his feet closer to the rest of his body to make room.

"Hey, Mom."

"Beautiful day," she said, and it was. The sun's rays made the grass look greener and the shade underneath the trees felt like paradise. "How does it feel to be home?"

Benny didn't describe how after six months on a nationwide tour with Stan and a short detour that turned into a three-month yo-yo training session that no place felt like home.

Instead, he said, "Feels good."

"You've got any plans Benjamin?"

"No, Ma." It felt like déjà vu. Back for four days and she was already getting on his case like he was an ambitionless slacker fresh out of college instead of an internationally renowned yo-yo performer.

"You've got some money in the bank, but that doesn't mean you should stop planning for the future. The future always comes."

"Yeah, it does." The waves were bringing him closer to the shore. "Mom, what are your plans for the future?"

"My plans? Well… hmmm, I want to see you and your brother and sister succeed."

"Those are your plans for us. What do you want for yourself?" She looked into the air, past the dragonflies and through their back door and then Benny's voice brought her back to their yard. "Just think about it, Ma. Give me an answer whenever you feel like it. I've got money and power now. I can make things happen. I'm sure as heck not going to be able to spend all this money on myself." That was as close as Benny could express his feeling that living life was becoming a chore. The average life expectancy for a white male was 74 years and Benny didn't know how he could possibly occupy those next fifty plus years. "When you were my age Mom what did you want to do?"

"Well, I never considered being a real estate agent. But you never know what life brings you. I've got one son who gets rich playing with a toy. Another child living in the worst place in the world and another child… urinating on my garden! Jimmy, what are you doing?"

"It's good for the plants, Ma. It's like fertilizer." Jimmy yelled as he zipped up his fly.

"I can't believe I raised a hillbilly. You know those are eggplants you peed on. In a couple months you're going to be eating them."

"It adds to the flavor."

Benny laughed at his brother's comment. It was good to be home. He didn't mean to stay those months with Mr. Pratt, but Ben couldn't bear to leave that old man in solitude again. Ben knew better than anyone how lonely loneliness could be. Besides Ben got to hone his yo-yo skills to a razor sharp edge, learn some more amazing details about the rules and history of the Yo-Yo Brigade, and he got to watch a lot of TV. But finally it was time to return to Hatchet City. Springtime there was glorious, and this year spring started early. Flowers blooming, sunshine zooming, and maybe Jenny would be back home.

"Hurry up. Dinner's getting cold." Dad yelled from the back porch.

Benny manipulated himself out of the hammock. He forgot his parents liked to eat so early. They each said eating too close to bedtime would give you some disgusting gas when you sleep. Benny enjoyed the predictability of home. The only surprises were Mom baking a spectacular apple pie and there being piles and piles of fan letters from people whose lives were touched by Benny's yo-yo. Amongst those greetings from strangers was a parcel more significant. No, it wasn't from Jenny. But it was postmarked from the other side of the world and carried a letter that read,

Benji,

Haven't heard from you in a while. If I didn't know you better, I'd think you had forgotten about me. Mom sent me that feature they wrote about you in People magazine. When I get back you're going to have to take me to all those celebrity parties including at least one at the Playboy mansion. Eight more months to go. It will go by quickly now that I'm starting to enjoy myself. I didn't want to admit to anyone how much I hated it here. It would have meant taking a thousand "told you sos" from everyone who thought Siberia was a nutty place to go. But to tell the truth, and I'm only telling you this because you already knew it since we share a cosmic twin consciousness, I was crying myself to sleep every night for months.

But no more because Betty James has actually fallen in love. Don't worry, he isn't some Soviet dogsledder. His name is Eric from Portland, Oregon, USA and he's a fellow Peace Corps nut. You'll dig him when you get to meet him. And don't you dare criticize him as much as I criticized Kim (even though I was right and she was a stupid girl who didn't know what she wanted). Eric and I already talk about getting married. I tell him we should wait and see what our relationship will be like under normal circumstances, when we're not completely alienated by the people around us. Then he'll say something dorky like, "You're the only thing that doesn't alienate me." He's the best. But enough gushing. Write back! Sharing cosmic twin consciousness is no substitute for actual mail.

Hugs and kisses,
Betty

The letter brought Ben happiness, jealousy, and indifference. And Dad brought Ben a big heap of mashed potatoes with mushroom gravy. They sat in silence drinking apple juice and eating seconds and thirds when Dad nudged Ben, "Did you hear about all the universities that accepted Jimmy?"

"Must be the sex appeal." Jimmy said.

The home cooking brought Benny back into his old self-depreciating habits. "Good. At least two of your children aren't losers."

Dad pointed his fork at Ben. "Don't you call your sister a loser. She traveled to a prison state on her own accord."

Benny had forgotten he was a success. Stan was already planning a second tour where they would be playing at the big time venues. Ben mopped up the gravy with some confidence and decided it was time to stop procrastinating. After two slices of pie he took the stationwagon out to Jenny's house.

He took all the same turns. Stopped at the same red lights. Listened to the same radio station even though its format had changed from classic rock to good time oldies. And then he parked on the curb in front of her house. Ben noticed Jenny's gray, little hatchback was parked in the driveway. He took a couple of really deep breaths and then knocked on the door. It was so hard, this thing called accomplishment. Footsteps meant a door was the only thing between Ben and a warm body. The door opened and there she was. Her hair had grown down to her shoulders and her eyelids were sleepier and she had gained some baby fat but it was Jenny. It was all too much. Ben lost his equilibrium and his eyesight and collapsed on her doorstep.

"Ben. Get up you loser." It was Stan Friendly's voice.

"Stan. What are you doing here? Where am I?"

"You're at the place you've been dreaming about all these months. At the doorstep of your lady love."

"What are you doing here?"

"I'm not here. I'm not really Stan. I'm your id or your superego. Definitely not your ego since you don't seem to have one. I could be your conscience or a devil. Worry about it later you nimrod. You've got your goal in front of you, now get up and score. Or at least open your eyes."

"My eyes?" Benny inquired as he opened them and saw an angel's face floating above him.

"Ben, you're alive?"

"I am now that I see you again Jenny."

She giggled. "Ben, I'm not Jen. What's wrong with you? I'm Michelle. We should get you to a doctor."

Ben took a closer look at her as he brought himself slowly to his feet. This wasn't Jen, it was her younger sister. But Michelle was really starting to look like Jen. Maybe she could... Ben quickly stopped that thought. He would not substitute his object of desire for a doppelganger again. "Is Jen here?"

"Nope and you're not altogether here either. Have you become a druggie since you became famous?"

"No. It was just a shock. I thought you were Jenny and... where is she? I need to talk to her. You see what a mess I am without her."

Michelle stood her ground. "I can't tell you."

"What do you mean you can't tell me? How much money will it cost? I'm rich and famous now. I can give you anything."

"Give me what you got in your pockets."

Benny emptied his left pants pocket. He opened his wallet and handed over thirty American dollars. Michelle counted the bills slowly and said, "Empty your other pocket."

"There's nothing in there."

"Come on I see a big lump. You've got something in there or else you're way too happy to see me." Ben took out his yo-yo. Michelle nabbed that too. "I'll tell Jen you were in town and were looking for her."

"How about I just wait for her and tell her that myself?"

"No good. She's out of town."

"Then give me her number and I'll smooth things out with her. I'm not going to be in Hatchet City for long. I'm going on tour again and I need to see her."

"She would never talk to me again if I did that. She's not too fond of how you treated her."

"I've changed. I really have."

"How about you leave me an itinerary of your tour dates and maybe Jen will show up at one of them." She was backing Ben out the door.

"OK. But could you tell her how much I've changed? And tell her... I love her. I really do."

"I believe you Ben." And for that too brief a second between Michelle uttering those words and her slamming the door, Ben could have sworn it really was Jenny he was talking to.

Monday, April 2, 1990
11:00 a.m.
Chapter Nineteen

"I really wish you would shave. At least let that lady put some make-up on you. You've got a big zit on the back of your neck."

Ben had his back to Stan, but the mirrors in the room gave the illusion that he was reflecting upon what Stan was saying. So Stan kept talking and Ben kept twirling his yo-yos around.

A young woman wearing headsets stepped into the dressing room to say, "You've got five minutes, Mr. James."

"Thank you," Ben said.

Stan paced around the tiny dressing room as he barked, "Remember to go over your nationwide tour, talk about the next tour dates, and make sure to mention Rebecca's new TV show. You still haven't agreed to a guest appearance. When do you want to do it?"

"Mmmmhmmm." Ben said as he picked up a bottle of water with his yo-yo.

"Why don't you listen to me anymore, Ben? Ever since you went out to the desert for those three months I feel like I'm talking to a ghost. That could have been you with a TV show. But since I couldn't find you, Rebecca has the show and all the residuals. What the heck did you do in the desert? Listen to me, darn it!"

The show's production assistant toned down the conflict by walking in and saying, "One minute."

Ben twirled his yo-yos around Stan's hands and pulled himself up. "I'm listening to you loud and clear, Stan." But Stan's words didn't affect Ben anymore. Those three months in the desert really did change Ben. All that time out there without human contact except for a crazy old man and cable television gave Ben time to believe maybe all he needed was himself. Himself and a yo-yo or something that would help kill the time. Ben walked down the corridor with a renewed sense of purpose. He would show the world yo-yos were all you need.

And Jonny Steele, talk show host extraordinaire gave Ben his introduction, "Our next guest is the 1989 world Yo-Yo Champion. He will be performing at the Sno-Cone in LA this Thursday and Friday and at Jerry's Place in San Diego on Saturday. Put your hands together for The Yo-Yo Kid, Benny James."

Benny didn't greet the audience's canned enthusiasm with words or jokes as Stan had taught him to do. His yo-yos came out violently and returned to his hands with such force, it was shocking. Every time the yo-yo left Benny's hands, the crowd flinched. They thought he wanted to hurt them. When he swung from a light fixture, it looked like he was trying to tear the roof down. For the finale Ben juggled three knives with his yo-yos and a lady in the third row recited a Hail Mary. But then Ben chopped his two gratuitous yo-yos and caught the three airborne knives with the only yo-yo that mattered, his trusty wooden Jenny. Ben bowed but only a couple astute people noticed the prompter was flashing applause.

Jonny Steele was too awestruck to get up, shake Ben's hand, and invite him to talk. So Benny took the initiative and walked right over to the couch. The acclaimed Czech film actress, Franka Rochenka, scooted over. Her dyed pink hair really caught Ben's eye. He gave her his Hollywood smile. Ben turned toward Jonny Steele before she had a chance to give a giggly smile back.

"Did you like it Jonny?" Ben asked the former action movie star who was turning his career around with a hit talk show.

"That was something else. I don't know if our audience at home could feel all the danger and passion you brought out here. But that was extreme. What are you thinking about when you do those tricks?"

"Love."

"Love? Now that must be some girl!"

"She is."

Jonny nodded his head at his producer who was signaling that it was time to wrap things up. "Well thanks a bunch for coming Ben."

"My pleasure."

"Benny James. Make sure to check him out ladies and gentlemen. I also want to thank Franka Rochenka. Go see her new movie *Dark*. It's sexy, sexy stuff. Tune in tomorrow when we'll have another great show. Until then I'm Jonny Steele wishing you peace and happiness."

As the house band played the closing credits music Jonny Steele rushed over and told Ben how talented he was. Then he told Franka how beautiful she was. Her reply was, "Stay avay from me." And Jonny Steele got lost.

Benny then made an attempt to chit-chat with the star. "So what movie are you in?"

Her accent was as thick as his Mom's berry cobbler. "It is called *Dark*. It is very intelligent. You might not understand it."

"What did you think of my yo-yo?"

"I found it interesting that you said love inspired you."

"Tell you what, if you're not doing anything tonight, we can have dinner and I'll tell you all about it."

"You are very sure of yourself for a man who plays vith toys."

"Am I?" Benny always thought confidence and him went together like horseshoes and ducks.

"Ve vill meet at Spandego's at eight." And with that she walked off to her dressing room.

Ben was too busy basking in glory to ask where the heck Spandego's was. There was also that pesky performance he was supposed to give at nine, but the fans could wait because Benny James had a five-star date. Woohoo!

Monday, April 2, 1990
6:03 p.m.
Chapter Twenty

First date. Can't be late. Gonna be great. Benny skipped in his rental car to Spandego's, a fashionable eatery down in the Sunset Strip. He was supposed to be at his gig in just under an hour, but this could be worth it. He parked his car with the valet and opened the double doors. Inside the furniture and walls were pitch black with Jackson Pollack paint drippings ruining everything. The waitress, waiters, and busboys were all wearing white work clothes with paint stains. And there she was, Franka Rochenka in her sunglasses and tight clothes that made her look every inch of the movie star that she was.

"You are late." She said not in ire, just matter-of-factly.

"I thought that was fashionable." No laughter. "Never mind. Let's grab a table."

Ben went over to the maitre d' handed him a two-dollar bill and was promptly seated. He looked at the menu and gasped. Nothing was under ten dollars. Franka ordered a seventy-dollar bottle of wine and a shiitake mushroom salad that ran at seventeen dollars. Ben ordered a bowl of Gazpacho soup for eleven dollars.

"And for your main course, sir?"

"That will be it. I'm on an... uh... all soup diet."

The waiter walked away and Franka said, "You may order more. I vill pay for your meal since I know you do not make as much money as I do."

"I make lots of money."

"As you vish."

He was suddenly sickened by her snootiness. Ben wouldn't let her beauty excuse her behavior any longer. "I make money. I just think it's wrong to waste all this money on food that probably isn't any good."

"Vhen you have been as poor as I, you learn money's only purpose is to be spent."

"Whatever." Ben sighed as he dug into the rolls. This was a big mistake. He wished he had not gone out and rented her movie *Final Episodes* this afternoon. It was the flick where a bored housewife played by Franka Rochenka was looking to connect with anyone. Ben felt her pain and wanted to give her that hug she so desperately needed, but the big screen TV was too darn wide.

The waiter set down her salad and his soup. Ben took one sip of the gazpacho and spat it out. "I told you this place is a rip-off. They can't even heat up the soup."

She laughed. The ice queen laughed a bit. "It is gazpacho. It is supposed to be served cold. You are joking, no?"

"Yeah sure I'm joking. Ha ha." He sank into the wine. He thought maybe he should let Franka pay since each sip was worth a dollar. She obviously wasn't what he was looking for. "You know Ms. Rochenka, I have a performance in about forty minutes. So maybe I should just pay now since this isn't working out."

"Vhat?"

"I'm sorry. I just don't see the point. You seem hellbent on humiliating me and even though you're beautiful to look at, your beauty isn't worth hurting my feelings… I wish you goodbye and good luck." He grabbed her hand and kissed her farewell. As he walked out the door he felt proud of himself. A lesser man would have given into lust.

"Ben!" That voice was almost familiar. But with that thick accent it could be no one but Franka. He prepared himself for a vicious slap, but instead was greeted with, "I am sorry. My behavior vas not inexcusable, but it vas rude. So I apologize." And now Ben had his chance to give her that hug. She accepted it and sunk into his shoulder like that was where she belonged. Ben imagined for a moment that maybe she saw him playing the yo-yo on TV and she felt a similar kinship to his loneliness.

"Would you like to see my show? I could get you a guest pass and a backstage pass too. It's lots of fun."

"Of course." She said and everything felt really comfortable. "Should ve both drive?"

"How about you drive? I don't know my way around town."

Franka gave the valet her card and he drove up in a noisy motorcycle. Franka put on a helmet and handed a spare one to Ben. He got on behind her, held on to the handles and the curve of her back felt just right. They gazoomed across town. Ben arrived just before the crowd got restless. As Stan and other men in suits swarmed Benny, Franka disappeared into the crowd. As invisible as an internationally acclaimed film actress could be she hid in the corner and shook her head as the lights dimmed, the disco music exploded, and Benny walked out in a leisure suit. She couldn't stop laughing at the indignity of the world's greatest yo-yoer doing a John Travolta from Saturday Night Fever impression. But her laughter stopped as the music changed and Benny undressed himself with his yo-yos. There would be no more music. Benny had decided the sounds the yo-yo made were as important as the sights. Once again she was amazed. Ben's hour went by faster than a New York minute. Before she could appreciate his brilliance for what it was, she was hollering along with everyone else for an encore.

Sunday, May 6, 1990
12:00 a.m.
Chapter Twenty-One

Love was grand. This time Benny even allowed himself the pleasure of enjoying it. Long walks and short kisses and crazy distances traveled just so they could spend some time together. It was almost enough to make Ben forget what's her name. But Jen's fate was a question he still needed answered, even if it didn't seem so important anymore. His new companion had so many interesting stories to share that Jenny seemed like a character in a book he had almost forgotten. Franka told him all about growing up Czech and about working for the sleazy director Edgar Enzo.

Then one evening in a hotel room outside St. Louis, they were watching cartoons. His arm wrapped around her back and her head laid on his shoulder. He turned his attention away from Popeye and tried to say the right words, "You know I think I might be crazy about you."

She smiled. She already knew he was. The way he cried in front of her when he felt his life was going nowhere.

"I'm so lucky I met you," he continued. "There was another girl I was once in love with. I really thought death would be the only way I could get over her. But then I met you."

He tried to keep his attention on Olive Oyl as he awaited her response. Then he almost missed it as she muttered, "I am another girl."

"What?"

"You already knew me before we met."

"Talk slower. I guess I still have trouble with your accent."

"I'm not Franka. I'm Jenny."

"What are you talking about? How do you know about Jenny?"

A tear she didn't intend on shedding appeared. "I vas born Jenny. Jennifer Jane Royce."

"That's impossible. Your lips are completely different." He said as he caressed them.

"Collagen."

He tore the sheets away from her. "Jenny didn't have such big... such a large chest."

"Silicone."

"What about your accent?"

"Hypnosis."

"And all those stories you told me about Prague?"

"Acting."

This was too much. He got up from the bed and looked for his clothes. "I don't know what game you're playing, but it's not fun. I don't know how you know about Jenny but forget about it."

She got out of the bed and Ben stared. He thought he was imagining all the similarities like he did for every other girl, but she put her arms around him and said, "Ve lost each other once. Let's not be stupid again. Let's talk before ve run avay and have any more regrets."

He knew she was right so they kissed and with perfect timing Popeye said on the television, "I yam what I yam."

Saturday, May 19, 1990
8:47 p.m.
Chapter Twenty-Two

"Benny Benny Benny Ben. We never get to talk any more."

Ben was backstage of Madison Square Garden. He sold the entire arena out. He was a pop culture phenomenon. A star on the magnitude of the sun and he wanted to keep his fans happy so he said, "I'm sorry Stan, we're always so busy. But right now I've got to prepare for my performance. Maybe afterwards?"

"Sounds fab." Stan said out of the side of his mouth. "How… how's your family Ben?"

"Well, Betty's due back from Siberia in a couple of weeks. Jimmy's getting ready for college life. Mom and Dad are the same as they ever were."

"Good… good. And how about Franka or Jenny or whatever that crazy broad calls herself nowadays?"

"She's great Stan, thanks for asking. How about your family? Has Veronica won any more beauty pageants?"

"No, Ben. She thinks she's too cool for that. She's into playing electric guitar now which is just as well. I want her to keep a low profile, I think your loved ones should too, know what I mean?"

"No, I don't Stan."

"Well, you're famous and people might take advantage of your fame and riches through your family. You know Frank Sinatra's son was once kidnapped and you're too young to remember Patty Hearst but a couple security guards wouldn't hurt matters."

"Have there been threats placed against my family?"

"No. No threats. More hints and allegations. It's nothing to worry about Benny. It's part of show business. Tell everyone to lay low and things will be fine." They stared at each other's chests when Stan patted down Benny's back and told him, "Forget about it. Go out there and knock New York dead."

Despite the fear and paranoia, Benny's automatic pilot was enough to give the people a show they would never forget. Benny James made the cover of Newsweek and his yo-yo, "Jenny", made the cover of Time. Everyone wanted a piece of him which was OK as long as no one took a piece out of anyone he loved. Benny knew it had to be Simon Wiesel who threatened him. It had to be that old coward. Benny hadn't been serving the public as a vigilante since Simon's stern warning months earlier. But maybe Ben was breaking some other arcane yo-yo law he knew nothing about.

Regardless, Ben made some plans for the people he held dear. His sister was safe in Siberia. His brother would be able to protect himself as long as he stayed on his toes. Mom and Dad were sent on an immediate cruise around the Caribbean Islands. And Franka/Jenny was ordered by Benny to come with him on his tour. She complained that would stall her burgeoning career. So Benny had Stan use his newfound show business clout to have Franka fired from the film she was hired to act in. The only thing Benny was sure of was that he could protect her.

So she cheered him on throughout his tour. After shows they dined in fine restaurants and slept in honeymoon suites. It was a great week. Then Benny performed his one man show, Benny & Jenny: A Man and his Yo-Yo in Denver, Colorado when disaster struck. Benny didn't start the day feeling too well. His fingers were stiff. He had them massaged and iced which didn't help, nor did Franka/Jenny's kisses.

The show had to go on so Benny showed the people what they needed to see. $27.50 for general admission or $43.25 for preferred seating the people got to see the endless possibilities of what a yo-yo could do. They also got to hear the blasts of a shotgun as six armed men wearing latex masks of Adolph Hitler took control of the crowd. At first it was generally believed that they were part of the show. Even Benny wondered why the choreography had changed without his permission.

But when he saw the barrel of a shotgun pointed at his beloved Franka/Jenny he knew all bets were off. One of the smaller Hitler masked men took Benny's microphone and announced to the crowd, "Benny James your hostile territorial actions have led us, The United Aryan Brotherhood of the Dragon to declare war on you until you surrender our property." A bullet would have messed Benny's shin up real bad if his yo-yo didn't serve as a shield. And with Franka/Jenny as a hostage the United Aryan Brotherhood of the Dragon fled the scene. Benny walked off the stage scared and anxious out of his head while the crowd clapped for more.

For the first time ever Benny actually wanted Stan to be waiting on the wings, but he wasn't there. Benny's maddening search eventually led Benny to his dressing room where his manager was sobbing like a wet baby.

"Stan, what happened?" Benny demanded.

"They took my baby. My Veronica. They took my little girl."

Ben wasn't impressed that his manager was in touch with his emotions. "Get yourself together. They took my girl too. They took Jenny." Benny hadn't even noticed that his trusty wooden yo-yo by the same name was now irreplaceably damaged by the bullet meant for his leg. "Who the heck is this United Aryan Brotherhood of the Dragon?"

"Ben, I'm so sorry I got you into this."

"Into what?"

"Well, remember when the money really started rolling in a few months ago and you said you had no idea how you could spend it all?"

"No."

"And then do you remember how I said I had a great place where you could invest your money and make a nice little return on it?"

"I don't remember any of this Stan. What does this have to do with the Aryan Brotherhood?"

"Well, I invested our money on this beautiful piece of property in Idaho. There are lakes and snowcapped mountains and shady pine trees. It was heaven, Benny, heaven. The previous owners of the land had stopped paying their taxes so the government seized the property and was selling it for a song. We bought the land thinking we could build a nice little resort and maybe a yo-yo theme park. How the heck was I supposed to know the reason the previous owners stopped paying their taxes was because they declared themselves a sovereign white supremacist nation?"

"So now they've kidnapped Jenny and your daughter in retaliation?"

"And my wife and your parents too."

"Golly Stan, is there anything else you feel like telling me?"

"No. I think that's all. I haven't talked to Simon yet…"

"Simon? Who's Simon?"

"We're rich Benny, but not that rich. I needed more capital to make our yo-yo resort a reality. So I brought in this kind senior citizen Simon Wiesel into our business plan."

"Simon Wiesel? Stan don't you remember that name?"

"Sure, he's a wealthy private citizen whose profile has been written up by many business journals."

"No! Don't you remember those vaudeville films you showed me at your house. Remember that Yo-Yo Kid. The one your um… grandfather screwed over. That's Simon Wiesel and he wants his revenge. There's no United Aryan Brotherhood of the Dragon. It's all an elaborate plot to hurt us."

"You think?"

"I know it," Benny said as he turned his back from Stan and walked toward the door.

Stan didn't like the idea of being left alone so he asked, "Where are you going Benny?"

"I'm going to save the day."

Sunday, May 27, 1990
8:45 p.m.
Chapter Twenty-Three

In the sticky bowels of Miami International Airport, Jimmy James was thoroughly discombobulated. In the last 24 hours he found out he got a D on his trigonometry final exam, his parents had been kidnapped by white supremacist terrorists, and his slightly deranged and overly famous older brother commanded him to get to the airport where a first-class ticket to Miami was awaiting him. Jimmy had been told after arriving to head to the baggage claim, even though he didn't check any luggage, and there he would receive further instructions. And just as Jimmy lost his patience a yo-yo wrapped around his waist and pulled him into a corner.

"Ben." It had to be his brother. And it was Benny looking very goofy in cheap sunglasses and a Gilligan Island hat. "What the heck is going on?"

"Shhh. Shut up and wrap one of these around each finger." Benny handed him two titanium yo-yos. "Let's walk. We shouldn't stay in any one spot for too long."

"Ben, have you lost your mind? What's going on?"

"Something serious. I trust you've been staying in tip-top yo-yo shape."

"Yeah, sure. Been doing Jack Pratt's stupid exercises."

"Good, then you should be of some use. Come on, I'm parked over here."

And in the corner of the carousel that commanded, "No parking any time" sat a shiny new rental car. Jimmy was about to take the front seat until he saw it taken by the television star, Rebecca Monet. Jimmy settled in the back, but as they drove away he demanded an explanation.

Rebecca also wanted to know, "What is going on?"

Benny finally started talking after he turned the radio on full blast. "Thanks for both coming out here without knowing why. I know who took my family and Stan's family hostage. Simon Wiesel. I found out where he is and I'm going to beat the stuffings out of that jerk."

"Who's Simon Wiesel?" Rebecca asked.

Jimmy filled her in on the origin of the original Yo-Yo Kid and then asked Benny, "What do you need us for?"

"I might need some back-up. He has at least six goons working for him. The most people I've ever taken on at once is four."

Rebecca laughed at what she assumed was a joke. When she saw he was serious, she really wished Benny would seek out some psychiatric help. She put her hand on his shoulder as he steered them towards the expressway. "Ben with all that has gone on the last couple days, you 're probably not thinking straight. With all the stress you probably shouldn't even be driving. Why don't we pull over, call the police, and tell them anything you know about the terrorists?"

"No. I'm going to hurt that old man." He sped up a little.

Jimmy smelled a whiff of dementia too. "Benny, maybe you should slow down a little. We've been through a lot the past couple days, but Mom, Dad, and your girl will be OK."

"Yeah, once I save them." As Benny said that Rebecca shot a truly concerned look to the back seat. They were being driven by a delusional maniac and she was worried for her life.

Benny followed the directions he had written on a napkin until they reached a middle-class residential area where stray cats arrogantly crossed the streets.

Rebecca asked, "Is this where your archenemy lives Ben? It doesn't look like much of a headquarters for an evil empire to me."

Benny ignored her sarcasm. He pointed at the clock on the dashboard and commanded, "You guys wait here. It's 9:21 if I'm not back by 9:40 come and get me."

He reached for the door when Rebecca yelled, "Ben." Benny turned his head just in time to be clocked by the titanium yo-yo he had given Rebecca an hour earlier. He was out cold and Jimmy was feeling really, really nervous. Jimmy grabbed his twin yo-yos and jumped out of the car. Rebecca jumped out after him and hollered, "Where do you think you're going?"

Jimmy was almost at a loss of words. Almost.

"Away from you, before you beat me up too."

"You've got nothing to worry about unless you start acting like a maniac too. You saw your brother, he was nuts. He might have just assaulted some innocent old man."

"Or he could have thwarted your boss' evil plans." Jimmy knew they were at a deadlock. Two strangers connected by an unconscious crazy. Jimmy had no choice. He was outmatched, so be brought his hand out to shake and asked, "Do you promise, you're on our side?"

She brought her hand out to shake and to say, "I promise." when Jimmy sucker punched her head with his titanium yo-yo. It knocked her back, but Jimmy had been lying when he told his brother he was doing his yo-yo exercises, so his thrust didn't have the power to knock Rebecca out. She swung her yo-yo at Jimmy, but she was seeing spots. Distracting spots that made her vision ugly, so Jimmy ran his yo-yo string around her, tied her up in a Boy Scout approved knot and threw her in the car.

With Benny out cold and Rebecca screaming obscenities, Jimmy decided to snoop inside the innocent looking house Benny was headed toward alone. Jimmy peeked through the front windows. No sign of life. He tried the front door, but it was locked, so Jimmy hopped over the wooden fence to get to the backyard. The screened pool deck was open so he snuck in and gazed through the sliding glass door into what could have been any elderly man's TV room. Framed pictures of grandchildren holding yo-yos, random medication containers laying around and a television tuned into game shows. Jimmy walked in making more noise than he intended, but no one came after him. He tiptoed around, not exactly sure what he was looking for. Then he heard a wailing cry that was as good a clue as any. He pushed open the door to a room drowning in the scent of vapor rub. An old, bald man looked up at him and whimpered slowly, "Go ahead and kill me."

Jimmy stood there speechless without any sense of what to do in a strange home in a strange town with a strange stranger making a strange request. "What are you waiting for? My time is up. Do me in."

"Are you Simon Wiesel?"

The sobs stopped for a second. "You know damn well who I am. Now hurry up Nazi, kill me, before I kick your heinie."

Jimmy almost laughed at this decrepit, old fossil kicking his heinie. But then the old man brought out his yo-yo at full force and Jimmy acted just fast enough to deflect it. Then another came and then another and Jimmy wondered how someone lying down could give a standing, strapping young man such trouble. As Jimmy struggled to defend himself, the old man held a conversation while unleashing an offensive threat. "You Nazis never could do anything right. You couldn't conquer Europe. You couldn't kill all the Jews. Your boss Hitler couldn't even grow a full mustache."

"I'm no Nazi." Jimmy yelled when he caught a breath.

The yo-yos kept coming. "Then who are you? And what are you doing in my bedroom?"

"I'm Jimmy James. Benny James' brother. He thought you kidnapped our parents and his girlfriend."

"Who? You Nazis are all interchangeable. I don't know your names."

"Benny James is The Yo-Yo Kid."

"I'm The Yo-Yo Kid. Oh you mean the phony, baloney Yo-Yo Kid." And he stopped his yo-yo attack. "You boys are Nazis? That Jackass Pratt sure knows how to align himself with some losers."

"No, dude. Me, Jack Pratt, and my brother got nothing to do with the Nazis. My brother thought you were working with the Nazis who kidnapped our parents and Stan Friendly's family."

"You come into my house and you talk about Nazis and the Friendly family?" Simon gave Jimmy a quick thwack in the noggin for such an indignity. "The Nazis killed the first Yo-Yo Brigade and after years of searching I find a couple new soldiers and the Nazis take them too. All because I let bygones be bygones and listen to a Friendly again."

Jimmy was not as patient as his big brother. He pretended to listen for three seconds, then he wormed his way out of it by saying, "Excuse me, Mr. Real Yo-Yo Kid, is it OK if I bring my brother in here. He might appreciate your yarn a bit more. Plus it would give you time to make yourself decent." The old man nodded and looked for his underwear as Jimmy left the house. Jimmy flicked his yo-yos a couple times to get back in Zen with his yo-yos. But then Jimmy felt one with worry when he spied that neither Rebecca nor his brother were waiting by the car. He ran back to the Wiesel household to avert Weird War III. And who was sneaking in through the back door, but a bruised and bloody Benny and Rebecca.

Jimmy greeted them with a combination of relief and anxiety. "What are you guys doing?"

"I'm going to kill that old man."

"And what about Rebecca knocking you out earlier?"

Benny looked at his brother and then at Rebecca. "What? I thought you said I slipped and hit my head."

The two brothers converged on her and she suddenly wished she never had followed Benny's request to come to Miami. She was all ready to defend herself when an old man's voice hollered, "Well if it isn't The Yo-Yo Kid and the Yo-Yo Hussy. Your show stinks you hussy."

She defended herself. "I don't write the show. I just act in it."

"Like what you do is acting."

With a full head of steam Benny walked up to his predecessor and demanded, "Why did you do it Mr. Wiesel? Why? I was finally happy and you had to ruin it."

"You were happy? I was happy. I finally had my brigade and then they took them away."

"Taken away? I'm glad someone took away your neo-Nazis."

Jimmy stood inbetween the crazed past and crazed present incarnations of The Yo-Yo Kid. "I think you should both start from the beginning. You too, Rebecca, how are you involved in this?"

She was outraged. "Well, what about you junior? I want to hear something about you."

"You want to hear about me Miss evil TV star? My parents are kidnapped, my brother is a deranged celebrity who called me to help him and all I know about you is you sucker punched my brother."

Rebecca was about to explain herself but was then relegated to the background as Benny told his story. "I was performing when some Nazis kidnapped my parents and Jenny. Stan Friendly told me it was because he bought the Nazis' homeland along with an investor named Simon Wiesel, a man who had previously kidnapped and tortured me."

"You call what I did to you torture? You are a sissyboy. Keep your hands to yourself and I'll tell you what I had to do with this." Mr. Wiesel said out of his wheelchair. "I'm sure Jackass Pratt told you my life story. And how Pratt and I had both been trying to restart The Yo-Yo Brigade. I had my two perfect, mindless soldiers. I even had a third, before that Jezebel standing behind you gave up on a noble calling when Stan Friendly threw a little money at her. Everything was going fine until I received a form letter from Stan Friendly. He didn't even know who I was, I bet he sent it to everyone with a large account at Friendly Bank. It invited me to invest in some land in Idaho where we would build a yo-yo theme park. I threw some money in because it sounded like a good isolated training ground for my Yo-Yo Brigade, but I should have known anything involving a Friendly is trouble."

Jimmy had to ask, "So no one in this room has anything to do with Nazis?"

"No," sang the chorus.

So Jimmy asked, "What are we going to do to get our family and Mr. Wiesel's mindless yo-yo soldiers back?"

Benny answered, "We can have Stan surrender the property deed back to them."

"Ahhh, I knew it. I knew you were a phony," Mr. Wiesel hollered.

That was the first of Simon's comments that really rubbed Ben the wrong way. "What do you suggest Mr. Wiesel?"

"I'm calling Jackass Pratt. He'll pick us up in the Yo-Yo-copter then the three of you will ambush those Nazis like a real Yo-Yo Brigade would."

Tuesday, May 29, 1990
2:23 p.m.
Chapter Twenty-Four

The light called to Benny so he approached it. Out of the light came a voice. "You're lucky you met me."

Benny couldn't argue. "You're right."

"Do you even know who I am?"

"Of course."

"Who am I?"

"I don't know exactly, but I'm sure I'm very lucky to have made your acquaintance."

And out of the light a dense object struck his head. "Mr. Wiesel?" Benny got hit in the head again so he kept throwing out names. "Mr. Pratt? Stan? Jenny/Franka?"

And the light said, "You almost got me figured out."

"Kim?"

And from the light came the slim, willowy silhouette of a yo-yo. "I'm Jenny. And you left me behind Benny. You could always find another girl to be your true love, but what about me? I've always been there for you, and you repay that by using me as a bulletproof vest and throwing me away like I'm nothing."

"I'm sorry about that. I just had too much going on. But you're not nothing. You're my yo-yo."

"I am your yo-yo. But I am also more than that." she said as she swung toward him. As the yo-yo swung so did Benny's entire plane of existence. It swung enough so that his eyes opened. There wasn't one yo-yo facing him, there were many. He was in the Yo-Yo-copter, a specially equipped helicopter financed by Jack Pratt years ago, in case he ever could produce an honest to goodness Yo-Yo Brigade.

And now there finally was a Brigade. Jack Pratt flew the chopper even though the state of Arizona wouldn't issue him a license to operate a motor vehicle. Simon Wiesel and his wheelchair were strapped up front while Benny, Rebecca, and Jimmy were licking their chops and biting their knuckles at the thought of taking on a militia with nothing but yo-yos. In the back of the Yo-Yo-copter sat Stan Friendly as quiet as Benny had never heard him.

Simon Wiesel insisted on inviting Stan. Benny didn't know what good he could be. Mr. Friendly was proficient with a yo-yo, but he clearly wasn't Yo-Yo Brigade material. But Mr. Wiesel's philosophy was you always had to give a man a chance to be a hero. And what more heroic chance would Stan ever have than saving his wife and daughter from white supremacist terrorists.

Benny had no idea the ride would take this long. Idaho never seemed so far away. He twirled his yo-yos and couldn't help but to miss Jenny. Both the yo-yo and the woman. Benny was so fixated on his sorrow that he missed seeing Mr. Pratt give up the reins of the Yo-Yo-copter to Mr. Wiesel. Old Mr. Pratt sat next to Benny with a smile on his face. "Are you excited Benjamin? You should be. Your whole life has led up to this moment."

That's funny, Benny thought. His whole life had led up to him feeling scared, confused, and helpless, but Benny kept those thoughts to himself as one of his many mentors dispensed more wisdom.

"Nothing makes you feel more alive than having something to fight for."

"No, Mr. Pratt, you're wrong." It didn't take Benny long to break his vow of silence. "Having someone to love makes you feel a whole lot more alive."

Jack Pratt showed off his dentures with a smile. "Benjamin, quit talking like that. Romantics always die young and I want you to come back from this mission healthy."

Simon Wiesel gasped over the loudspeaker, "Jackass Pratt quit your yakking. We are almost there. Prepare the Yo-Yo-vator for the Yo-Yo Brigade."

Mr. Pratt stood up slowly and prepared the Yo-Yo-vator, a giant yo-yo that the four soldiers would strap to their bodies. Slowly the Yo-Yo-vator descended from the Yo-Yo-copter and the Yo-Yo Brigade unstrapped themselves and jumped the last ten feet to the ground. The

Yo-Yo-vator stayed in a sleeper position for a short minute and then wound back up to the Yo-Yo-copter.

Benny, Stan, Jimmy, and Rebecca picked themselves up from their awkward drop and watched the silent blades twirl into the horizon. Benny tightened his heavy pack filled with canteens, a water purifier, concentrated protein meals, mayonnaise sandwiches, spare yo-yo parts, walkie-talkies, and heavy duty explosive yo-yos in case something needed to be blown up.

"What the heck were we thinking?" Stan whined as Benny took inventory.

Benny shrugged his shoulders and started the long hike. "I don't know Stan. What were you thinking when you provoked this?" Stan didn't have the time or the peace of mind to respond. The Brigade was escaping him, so Stan did less talking and more walking through the wooded preserve.

The four soldiers had absolute faith in their map of the area surrounding the nation of The United Aryan Brotherhood of the Dragon that Mr. Wiesel obtained for them. Unless the Brothers kept the hostages outside, the map showed there were only three compounds where they could be hidden. Benny kept imagining what he would do to the scoundrels who planned this until the sun started its long descent, then he helped set up camp. They ate their mayonnaise sandwiches and Stan suggested to Ben, "How about a fire?"

"No. They might spot the smoke."

"How do we even know we're headed in the right direction, Ben? Just a few days ago you were crowing in my ear that the old geezer was behind the kidnappings. How do you know getting the two of us lost wasn't the final nail in his grand revenge scheme?"

It made too much sense but Benny's hatred would dissipate if he had to keep focusing it on a new target. "No, that's impossible. Mr. Wiesel can't be that smart and manipulative. Besides Jack Pratt would have nothing to do with hurting me."

"How do you know old man Wiesel isn't manipulating old man Pratt and is planning on strangling him once they land the helicopter. Ever think about that smart guy?"

"No I haven't Stan. But sometimes… sometimes you have to have faith in people." Benny said with a paranoid shiver before covering his body with leaves. "I'm going to get some shut eye. We've got a big day tomorrow, so I suggest you do the same." And as Benny recited the mantra he always sang when preparing to meet the Sandman alone, Stan stood up. He walked towards the other Yo-Yo Brigadiers, but then kept walking as he saw they were involved in their own private conversation.

"I'm a bit worried about tomorrow." Jimmy confessed as he leaned against the same tree as Rebecca.

"I am too Jimbo," Rebecca said as she limbered her yo-yos.

"You realize we could die tomorrow?"

"I know that. There's a chance we could even die tonight."

"Exactly, so why waste right now." Jimmy said and Rebecca looked at him in a way that he knew she knew where the conversation was headed. So his tongue headed straight for her lips and his hands went towards her bosom and her yo-yo slammed right into his ear.

She stood back and drew a line in the dirt with her yo-yo. "I'm going to sleep now Jimbo and in the morning we'll forget this ever happened. But if you cross that line tonight, it won't be no United Aryan Brotherhood of the Dragon that issues you a death warrant." Rebecca tucked herself into the leaves and guffawed at what her current bodyguard/boyfriend Bronson would do if he caught that skinny college boy putting the moves on her.

Jimmy found himself some leaves and went to sleep on the ear that wasn't ringing. Stan, meanwhile, stood there watching the sun slide below the trees to the almost inaudible sound of Benny repeating the same words over and over. "Jen. Jen. Jen. Jen."

Wednesday, May 30, 1990
6:22 a.m.
Chapter Twenty-Five

Standing in the middle of a rugged trail was a pristine, white kitten. Clean kittens don't live in the wild, so they had to be close. And as they passed the cat she spoke to them. Or rather he spoke to them since it sounded exactly like Stan Friendly's voice and what he said was, "Meow. Meow. Meow." On the third meow Rebecca awoke. She shook off her leaves and looked for Stan. She wanted to tell him how he would look if he was a cat. But Stan was nowhere to be found. She ran over to Ben, woke him up. Ben's yo-yo came half an inch from breaking her face. It didn't stop Rebecca from breaking the news that, "Stan's missing."

"He probably went to use the bathroom."

"His knapsack's gone too."

Ben stood up to a headrush that prevented him from immediately worrying about all the trouble Stan's going AWOL could cause. He began disassembling camp leaving Rebecca clueless as to what they should do. The fearless leader walked over to his brother, kicked him awake, and then he spoke, "Let's get going, Jimmy. Stan's missing if he's not here by the time we're ready to leave, we leave anyway." And a couple of tense minutes of packing later, they had no choice but to get up and go go go.

Even though the air was crisp and the landscape as sweet as butter, Jimmy couldn't help but to complain. "Why did they have to drop us off so far away?"

"So the evildoers wouldn't see us coming. The element of surprise and our yo-yos are the only things we have going for us."

"I think your brother's got another reason for having us walk so far." Rebecca charmingly added. "It's real easy for Benny to love this Jenny chick as long as she's a good distance away. That way she's the perfect ideal figure that is so easy to love. But once they really are together Benny will see Jenny's got her own flaws and problems."

"Benny's always had intimacy problems."

"And that's why your brother does all these crazy things to delay the inevitability of actually getting to know this girl he likes to call his true love. Because Benny still hasn't figured out the difference of loving the idea of love and actually loving a person. At least that's what my therapist said."

"Maybe that's what you need Benny, a little therapy."

"Chyuk hyuk hyuk." Benny mocked laughter and without turning around grumbled, "Maybe what you need is a trip to the hospital if you keep talking." Benny walked another minute spouting curse words in his head before he confronted Rebecca. "And what the heck are you talking to your therapist about me for? Especially when you have no idea of who I am. If you can't see how much I love Jenny/Franka than..."

"Benny, can't you see you can't be in love with someone if you don't know what to call her."

"Jeez Louise! This is a life or death situation we're walking into. This is not the time for you to tell me to get in touch with my feelings."

Rebecca stayed silent for a second. Then in a stage whisper to Jimmy she added, "Again he runs from his problems."

"Let's just shut up and walk." Benny yelled. How the heck could she question his love for Jenny/Franka? He knew she had flaws. He knew Jenny/Franka better than he knew himself and she was everything that is good in the world. And so he walked almost at peace through the gorge and between the Square Dance Mountains and past the first of many signs with a dragon insignia that read, "Private property. No trespassing." The map had been completely correct up to that point. They were now within the United Aryan Brotherhood of the Dragon's borders, so they moved much more quickly and deliberately.

Then they heard footsteps. The Yo-Yo Brigade got silent so they could observe two Brothers with shotguns hunting for some kind of game. Whether the game was human or animal Benny could not say.

When the hunters passed the Yo-Yo Brigade continued their march. Forty minutes later they reached Dragonia, the glorious trading hub of the United Aryan Brotherhood of the Dragon. Dragonia was a slum of ramshackle log cabins each bearing the distinctive stars, circles, and triangles of the United Aryan Brotherhood of the Dragon's national flag. A foul stench floated in the air since the citizens of Dragonia unanimously voted to spend their sewage allocation on more guns. Upon these initial observations the Yo-Yo Brigade retreated into the forest. Benny told them what their next steps were.

"We're going to set up camp and get some rest. When the sun goes down we'll snoop around and find the hostages. You guys will take the hostages back to the rendezvous point and I'll beat the crud out of the scum who masterminded this."

Jimmy was too exhausted from the hike to talk any sense to his brother. He found leaves, dug himself a hole and captured forty winks.

Thursday, May 31, 1990
4:13 a.m.
Chapter Twenty-Six

The food was the final indignity. Being locked in a chicken coop with six other people without a toilet? Fine, she could take that. Being humiliated and threatened by their inbred guards? Fa, she had dealt with more vile cretins in Hollywood. The loss of freedom? Freedom's just another word for nothing left to lose. But this cooked gruel they served was the final straw. For the previous two months Franka Rochenka had been seduced by the raw food diet. She could now taste the death in anything cooked. All the vitamins and minerals and life force are baked away. She had explained that fact over and over with her captors. "Don't you have any salads or fresh fruit, you monsters. You stupid creatures have no..."

"Shh, Franka, shh." Susan James, Benny's Mom put her hand over Franka's mouth. "Don't you see the way the guard looks at you?"

"Vich vun?"

"The one with his hand in his pants."

"Vich vun?"

"The one with the mustache. I don't think you want to give him an excuse to try sedating you."

"You are right." Franka took a seat on the muddy floor. After five days in these rough conditions, she no longer cared about staining her original Zapata dress. She looked in the corner and saw Benny's father Henry playing with the chickens. Cindy Friendly was letting her daughter, Veronica, sleep on her lap. And the two yo-yo nerds, Edgar Jones and Javier Hernandez, were in the back planning something very hush hush. "Do you think ve vill make it out alive Mrs. James?"

"I'm sure we will young lady."

"You do not care for me, do you?"

"Oh no. I'm sure you are a very lovely girl. I just don't believe that you really are Jenny from Hatchet City."

"Vhy vould I lie?"

"I don't know, why would you? I'm sure it would have nothing to do with Ben being extremely rich."

"I am vealthy enough so that I need no man's money."

"Sure. I'm sure you're very well compensated for your work in pornography. But it never hurts to strike some more oil."

"How dare you? If you vere not Ben's mother I vould scratch out your eyes."

A shrill whistle broke up the conflict as the non-mustached guard walked over. "Listen ladies, much as I like to see a catfight, Cletus and I got our orders to keep you quiet while they work on negotiations. So keep a muzzle on your mouths."

"Filthy pigs," Franka muttered under her breath.

Meanwhile in the outskirts of Dragonia, the Yo-Yo Brigade was seeking to complete its first mission. The three adventurers hugged the long shadows and let their infrared goggles do their seeing for them. They kept their collective cool and skipped from building to building looking for their people. Then behind a corner they heard movement. Benny gestured for his two underlings to stay still while he took a gander. It was a Brother of the Dragon with a shotgun strapped to his back. Against his better judgment Benny bonked the Brother in the back of his head with one yo-yo and dragged him by the neck with another yo-yo to his posse. "I caught myself a dragon." Benny told them as he walked them into the woods.

"Where are they?" Benny asked the Brother between punches. "Where are the people you kidnapped?"

"I don't know." The Brother insisted as he spat out a tooth.

"Then you're no good to us." Benny took out a Swiss army knife which looked monstrously dangerous to their captive.

"Alright. I'll take you to them."

"No," Benny said. "Show us on the map." And the Brother pointed to chicken coop 13. Benny then tied the Brother with titanium yo-yo string and filled his mouth with dirt and leaves and covered it with masking tape.

Benny then led his troop to its rightful glory. But as they walked Benny had to shake out his right hand. Mr. Pratt was right about only using the yo-yo as a weapon. If a yo-yo breaks against a hard head, then you can always buy another, but if your hand breaks the Lord only gave you one spare.

Then in front of his eyes stood chicken coop 13. In there was all the love he ever and never imagined. "I'm going in there to rescue them. Don't come in unless you hear me clucking like a chicken."

"How does a chicken cluck?" Jimmy asked.

Benny gave him a stare and then crawled into his destiny through a hole in the barn's wall. His shoe got stuck in a loose plank and to free himself he tugged his foot. It made a great bang which caused the chickens to all ruffle their feathers. And a Brother yelled from afar, "Shut your mouths."

Benny was never so glad to see a bigot with a gun. No way these guys would be armed just to guard livestock. He looked around the barn and there in the corner he saw her. Muddied and bloodied she still looked beautiful. She and the other hostages including Mom and Dad were trapped in a locked wire coop. Benny didn't even need those explosive yo-yos. All he needed were wirecutters or a razor sharp yo-yo blade! Benny crawled to the coop and sliced a nice sized hole.

He whispered, "Pssst!"

No one woke up so he "pssst" a bit louder and his Mom rubbed her eyes, "Benny, what are you doing here?"

"I'm rescuing you. Wake everyone up and get them out of here."

"Yes, sir." His Mom said in the same tone she used whenever her ungrateful son barked an order at her.

One by one the hostages awoke and crawled away. Each one stopping to thank Benny from the bottom of their hearts. He got lots of hugs and deep, deep gratitude, but he didn't want any part of it. Then it was Franka/Jenny's turn. She put one arm around him and then another and as much as this was what he always wanted he had to tell her, "Not yet. This isn't over."

"But you saved me."

"Yeah, but now I need to find the people who did this to you and make sure this never happens again."

"But you saved me from them doing anything. There's no need for revenge. Ve are together."

"Go with the others. This is the way it has to be done." She did as she was told because this was not the carefree young man she had such fond memories of. This was a bitter soul she did not recognize. And for a second Benny also wondered when everything had changed. When did selfish vengeance take precedence over getting a good, wet kiss from his girl? But that second passed and Benny went out looking for trouble.

He grabbed the two sleeping Brothers that were guarding the prisoners by their necks and left them a breath from the afterlife. The one with the mustache was hyperventilating, so Benny asked him, "Who's your leader?"

"The United Aryan Brotherhood of the Dragon has no leader. We are a confederation of brothers. Decisions are made democratically."

Benny smashed the politically conscious hatemonger in the left eye with his razor sharp yo-yo. "Who's the figurehead? Who's your founder? Who planned this kidnapping? Give me a name. Any name."

The beat-up Brother shook from the blood dripping from his eye. "Peter Dragon. Peter Dragon."

Before Benny could ask where Peter Dragon was, his informant had passed out. Benny went outside where dawn was breaking. He wondered how close the hostages were to the rendezvous point. Then he found himself a Brother. A big, hulking Brother that Benny hoped had his answers. "Where does Peter Dragon live?"

The brute reached for his gun, but Benny chopped off his trigger finger with the razor-sharp yo-yo and suddenly Benny had himself a stool pigeon. The nine-fingered Brother walked Benny to the Temple of Law where Peter Dragon resided. And as a reward the guide was tied to a horse's hind legs.

Benny walked into the dark cabin and in the short corridor there was a wooden door with a name scratched into it, "Peter Dragon."

On the other side of the door boomed laughter.

We'll see how long they laugh with yo-yos tied around their necks, Benny thought. Then he counted to two and kicked open the door. There was a split second for Benny to survey the situation. Two people were seated at a desk, but Benny went after the four standing guards first. One of the guards had been knocked down by the door bursting into his back, so Benny clocked him in the head to keep him out of commission. Then he grabbed two of the guards by their necks. The third guard ran over to attack Benny from behind but tripped over his fallen comrade. And Benny couldn't help but feel proud of how quickly he defeated four armed men until he heard the cock of a shotgun and a mysterious voice. "Fellow, I recommend you start praying to any Gods you hold dear."

"The only praying I'll be doing Mr. Dragon is that your children don't take your death too hard." Ben said exactly as he rehearsed it.

Then came a familiar voice. "Ben. Take a seat. I have this under control."

It was then that Ben noticed the other man seated at the desk was none other than Stan Friendly. "Stan! If you have anything to do with this I'll kill you too."

"You think I would have anything to do with kidnapping my own wife and daughter? Have a seat, Ben. We're conducting business."

"Business?"

"Yes business, Benny. I've negotiated our families' freedom. In exchange we're going to allow the United Aryan Brotherhood of the Dragon to keep their land that has already been settled. Now we're just trying to negotiate what percentage of Yo-Yo World Dragonia collects."

"I keep telling you, my Brothers will spit at any figure lower than 2.5 %."

"I understand Peter, but I won't continue negotiating until you put the gun away. It represents bad faith."

Peter Dragon unloaded his gun and then a smile came to his face. "I reckon you're Benny James. I've seen you on the TV. I really like your work. You ain't a Jew though, are you?"

Benny gave him his meanest stare. Then turned to Stan and said, "What are you doing? These guys are terrorists."

Stan's face flushed with red. "You'll have to excuse my associate, Peter. He's a bit wet behind the ears in the ways of commerce. Can I talk to him in private, Peter?"

Peter nodded letting the two of them step over the unconscious Brothers into the corridor. This was a mistake because before Stan could tell Benny what he was planning Benny said, "Stan, on the count of three run with me. One..."

"What?"

"Two... three." And as Benny sprinted off Stan had no choice but to follow. As Stan's sides really started to wheeze, he was glad he had followed for Benny's exploding yo-yo went off in Dragonia's Temple of Law. And Benny kept running and running and running past his Mom and Dad. Past Stan's wife and daughter. Past his brother Jimmy. Past his peers and rivals Rebecca, Edgar, and Javier. Past his lady love, Franka/Jenny. And there he was running all alone with no destination, no goal but continued survival. He ran past everyone but himself. No matter how fast or hard he ran, he never could escape Benny James and everything that came along with that identity. And so he stopped and caught his breath. He inhaled the morning air and as much as he thought he was too exhausted for human emotion, tears streamed from his eyes. Tears that proved Benny was no longer a wooden puppet, he was now an honest to goodness boy.

Then the blue fairy dropped the Yo-Yo-vator from the Yo-Yo-copter hovering above. One by one the rescued hostages were strapped aboard. Benny had no time to talk to each person he saved. Not even to Franka/Jenny who shot Benny a great smile. Benny looked away from it and her smile slowly cocooned into a sorrowful butterfly. Finally Benny attached himself to the Yo-Yo-vator which swung them up to the Yo-Yo-copter as they flew away.

"Way to go Yo-Yo Brigade." Simon Wiesel cheered as he saluted his two newly freed soldiers.

Jack Pratt put the Yo-Yo-copter on autopilot and handed all the hungry hostages mayonnaise sandwiches. Franka/Jenny scowled at hers as Mr. Pratt put his arm around Benny. "I knew you could do it Benjamin."

But he couldn't do it. There she was, his girl and he was scared of her. Scared of a future without desire. A future where everything he wanted was at his fingertips. Then Dad walked up to Benny and gave him such a hug. "I'm so proud of you, Benny."

"Thanks, Dad."

Then Dad turned his attention to Mr. Pratt, "So you're the man in the desert who taught Benny all about everything? So wise one, where are you flying us now?"

Mom came over and added her two cents, "I think since eight of the thirteen people on this helicopter..."

"It's a Yo-Yo-copter."

"Sure, Mr. Pratt. Well since, so many of us on the Yo-Yo-copter make Hatchet City our home that's where we should go."

"I am afraid that is not in the cards." Mr. Wiesel said with his two mindless lackeys lurking in the background. Benny got his titanium yo-yos ready for one more fight until Mr. Wiesel added less diabolically, "Because today is Jackass Pratt's birthday, so he gets to choose our destination."

Mr. Pratt looked embarrassed at everyone's cheer toward him, so Susan James took command. "That settles it. We're going to Hatchet City. The party will be at our house. How old are you Mr. Pratt?"

"I can't remember."

At that instance was when Benny felt the tap on his shoulder. "Ve need to talk."

Benny turned his attention to her. All dirty and a mess. This couldn't be what he always looked for. "Your mother does not think I am Jenny. She thinks I am a money-grubbing harlot. You don't believe I am Jenny either?"

"No, I don't." She slapped him and started crying. "I know you were Jenny. You've got that same mole on your stomach. But you have transformed into something else."

"You have too."

"Yeah, I've had a whole lot of plastic surgery, haven't I?"

"It's not that."

"Well, is it the fact that I tell everyone I am Czech when I've never even left the country?"

"No, it is much deeper."

"Is it that I've..."

"Shut up! Shut up!" she screamed. Benny did shut up along with everyone else in the Yo-Yo-Copter. "Can't you see how different you are too? Never in my life had I heard sarcasm from you. And now you hide your innocence and ven you talk you are so confident in yourself...."

Wait! Could this possibly be true. "Do I really sound confident?" And that simple, silly question made her laugh her Jenny laugh. Benny looked into her eyes, saw the truth. "I guess you're right. Time changes everyone. So now we've got to get to know each other all over again."

And then they kissed.

Not just any kiss. It was a kiss so loud with passion that everyone on the Yo-Yo-copter took notice.

Jimmy started the catcalls and applause and then everyone else joined in.

Thursday, May 31, 1990
7:22 p.m.
Chapter Twenty-Seven

Mr. Pratt had counted the years for everyone and had come to the conclusion that he was seventy-nine years old. That made him seven years younger than Simon Wiesel who officially passed down the mantle of Yo-Yo Kid to Benny.

While Mom was trying to piece together Mr. Pratt's insane recipe for a mayonnaise birthday cake, the Birthday Boy sat next to Benny and dispensed some more worldly advice. "See Benjamin, it's like I always told you, life is like a yo-yo. Sometimes it's up and sometimes it's down, but as long as it keeps spinning you're in good shape."

With slight hesitation Benny informed today's honoree, "Mr. Pratt you've never said anything like that."

"I didn't?" He looked around the room and sipped into his eggnog. "Well now it has been said."

The doorbell rang at the conclusion of that thought and Mom yelled, "Will somebody get that?"

Benny jumped at an excuse to stretch his legs. Without asking who was there, he swung open the door. And there she was with a suitcase in her hand. After all this time he was glad to see he hadn't made her up.

"Hey Benny." It was his twin sister Betty. "Are you going to just stand there or are you going to give me a hug and tell me why there's a helicopter in our front yard?"

He hugged her.

And later over a slice of mayonnaise cake, he explained that it wasn't a helicopter parked on their front lawn. It was a Yo-Yo-copter.

THE END

Sunday, May 2, 2021
1:33 a.m.
Bonus Chapter

"Benny." Jenny woke him up. After all these years Benny was still glad to hear Jenny have her Hatchet City accent again. "You know how it feels right now?"

"No."

"There was this song, I can't remember what it was, but it always reminded me of being a character in a book."

"Which character?"

"All of them. Any of them. But what gets me is the song really felt like what the characters' lives must be like after the words, "The End" flashed on the page."

"After people stopped reading about them?"

"Yeah." Jenny nodded.

"What did that feel like?" Benny really wanted to know.

She smiled, "Happy. It makes me feel happy."